BATTLE EARTH VII

NICK S. THOMAS

First published in the United Kingdom
by Swordworks Books.

ISBN 9781909149236

Typeset by Swordworks Books
Printed and bound in the UK & US
A catalogue record of this book is available
from the British Library

Cover design by Swordworks Books
www.swordworks.co.uk

BATTLE EARTH VII

NICK S. THOMAS

PROLOGUE

The war to survive had been won, for humanity to continue existing. The World must now find a way to live with one another in a newfound peace.

Ridding the planet of the alien invaders had been the aim of every human being since the first shot was fired, but it had not happened. Prisoner of War camps across the World were filled with alien combatants who had been trapped on Earth.

Demiran had been defeated by Mitch Taylor's own hand, a definitive stroke that made all who saw or heard of it believe the nightmare of alien contact was over; but not for Taylor. With no war to fight, his superiors found new ways to exploit his name and fame.

'What to do with the alien prisoners of war?' was the question on many minds, but even as they thought it, a new threat was looming. A threat that Taylor had only begun to get an insight to and the only one among them that understood, lay in a coma. The danger no longer came from the enemy at their gates, but the enemy within.

CHAPTER ONE

Tsengal lay still on the hospital bed where he had been for the last four years. His heart was still beating, but there was little other sign of life. Taylor visited him whenever he could. He wondered like they all did what memories lay in the alien's head.

Does he dream of Chandra's death? he asked himself.

He certainly did and he wasn't even there. He could still only speculate as to Chandra's fate, but it seemed all but certain she was dead. And yet, mystery surrounded Tsengal's return, and what he'd tried to tell them before he passed over to unconsciousness.

"You won't make him wake by hoping for it."

Taylor turned and saw Jafar a few steps behind him.

"Will he ever wake up?"

"I have said this many times. He'd have been finished off. Years of this 'coma' as you call it would be considered a waste where we came from. But I have told you this countless times."

"I know, but he needs to wake up."

Jafar nodded in agreement.

"We have to get to work."

Taylor turned, accepting there was nothing else for it. Two guards stood on duty at the entrance to the room, both wore the insignia of the 2nd Inter-Allied. Taylor didn't trust anyone else with the security of their comrade.

"What time are we due on stage?" he asked Jafar.

"1300 hours."

Taylor groaned.

"This is really getting old."

"At least you don't have to wear the Mech suit."

He smiled in response. Jafar had taken on some of Jones' sarcasm that he so missed since the Captain's retirement. They stepped out and saw the face of a man who was quickly becoming Taylor's most annoying acquaintance.

"Come on, Mitch, we've got work to do. You've gotta be on stage in a half hour. Chop, chop!"

Taylor stopped in his tracks and glared at the man. He wore a perfectly cut and pressed suit. He'd never served in the military, and while Mitch had never cared to ask, he would bet his right arm he sat out the war in a comfy house somewhere far from the apocalyptic carnage they had all witnessed. That was Richard Weaver, his government appointed press and liaison officer.

"Look...Dick," he took a little pleasure in seeing the man's face tighten with scorn at the nickname. "I couldn't give a rat's ass what you want. I'll get up there because my country asks it of me, but what comes out of your mouth is worth less than shit."

Weaver looked taken aback. It was clearly one of the few times anyone had dared offend him, and he was unsure how to respond. He was a pencil pushing, slimy, backstabbing weasel of a man who Taylor had zero respect for. He was almost as tall as Taylor and clearly in healthy shape. He could have served and fought for their planet and their survival, but he chose to be selfish, and that was unforgiveable. He had a perfectly slicked parting and a tan that could only be the result of careful planning. He had make up applied which was as subtle as a news anchorman, and a Cartier pen placed in his upper suit pocket the same way every time. A matching branded tank watch on his wrist and a sleazy smile to top it all off. Getting nowhere with the Colonel, he turned his attention to Jafar.

"You big guy, you've gotta be suited up. You know the drill, get to it!"

Jafar looked as impressed by his tone as Taylor was.

"Don't forget who you work for now. You're an asset. You get to live a free and great life because of us. Now get to work."

With those words, Weaver paced off as if he'd laid down his orders and there was nothing more to say on the subject. They both knew they had to do the job, but being treated like dirt when they were going to do it anyway left a bitter taste in Taylor's mouth.

"Is this the kind of life you looked forward to and fought for?" asked Jafar.

Taylor shrugged his shoulders.

"Then maybe the next war will come soon."

* * *

Taylor approached the podium from where he was to begin. He was fully geared up in the latest make of Reitech armour. He was ten seconds late, and as he walked in to a cheer from the crowd, he caught sight of the scornful look on Weaver's face. Mitch smiled in response, and that only infuriated him. He lifted his hand, and the room fell silent. Hundreds of cadets looked on at their hero and hung on to his every word and motion. They could not get enough of the officer who killed Demiran in personal combat.

"Afternoon to you all," he stated, making an informal salute to them, "Millions fought and died in the wars with the invaders. I bet most of you saw little of the war, and consider that a blessing, for you were too young to fight it. But now you're being forged into the next generation of fighters, the next marines!"

Roars of applause followed.

"Long after officers like me are too old to still wear a combat uniform, you men and women will carry the torch, and you have a lot to live up to."

A projection lit up behind him displaying images of some of his fallen comrades. Firstly, Colonel Chandra filled the screen, and a narration boomed out and echoed around the room to accompany the footage.

"Colonel Chandra, Captain Friday, just two of the many heroes who fought to save our planet from complete destruction. Remember them, and follow in their footsteps to greatness."

Taylor shook his head, a gesture that didn't go unnoticed by Weaver. His fallen comrades were being used as a cheap recruiting ploy, and it didn't sit well with him at all. He was in half a mind to jump from the stage and crack Weaver's jaw, but he refrained. He looked over to Jafar as the video continued and could see he looked no more impressed. His alien friend stood off to the side outside of the audience's view. He wore a full Mech suit, but the head cover plate was removed to reveal his face.

The video came to a close with a roar of applause, but it seemed a hollow gesture.

These kids don't know anything about what they've just been told, to them Chandra is nothing more than a character in a book. But, on the other hand, the potential future of the Corps is standing before me, and it's my duty to give them a good show.

"The alien invaders were a strong enemy which must

never be underestimated. Should you ever meet one, you want to be sure of your Marine training and weapons, for they will keep you alive. The Mech warrior is unlike any enemy our race has ever had to fight!"

He pointed to Jafar as he finished, and his friend stomped onto the stage in the towering and bulky Mech battlesuit. Gasps rang out, for they both knew the crowd had never seen a Mech in person, only on the TV and in video games.

"The first time I ever saw one of these was on the Lunar Colony. Just one single enemy soldier, and it took a platoon to take it down! Our bullets barely scratched it. They were terrifying war machines, the likes of which we had never seen!"

He lifted up a pistol from the display table beside him and fired two shots at Jafar. One ricocheted off and made a loud crash as it hit a clear shield that lay between him and the audience. It ruined the effect a little now they knew they were sheltered, but they still recoiled in surprise.

"Imagine the day we first stood before these metal monsters. Never seen an alien before. Never been in space before. Years of training for combat and being prepared for the next war, and it was nothing like anyone on Earth could have predicted. Faced with a technologically superior enemy we could barely hurt, we gave it our all. We lost many marines that day, and a great many more in the coming years, and yet today we stand triumphant because of the hard work of the men and women out there, with a rifle in hand. That marine could be you."

An image projected up before him of a press photo of a marine in full Reitech equipment and a corny grin on his face. He couldn't believe anyone would buy into it, but then, after all, he did. He continued.

"The heavily armoured Mech is not as slow as you may think, but they are heavily armoured and present large targets. When the great Marcus Reiter developed a new range of handheld weaponry which could take on this new threat, the war finally began to turn."

He picked up the huge Reitech rifle of which he had become so acquainted and lifted it. As he did so, a Mech suit was wheeled in remotely, propped up like a mannequin. It had several battle scars already that had been patched over for the display. He wondered for a moment if he had met its previous owner and sent it into whatever afterlife the aliens may imagine.

"When you have a relentless enemy coming at you, and all that you have left to rely on is your training and your equipment, pray that it is one of these in your hands!"

He lifted the rifle to his shoulder and fired two shots. The muzzles flashed the room in a strobe fashion, and the two rounds punched gaping holes in the armour. The crowd sighed and gasped before laughter followed, as if they were watching the latest outrageously unbelievable action movie.

"Sick!" someone in the crowd yelled out.

Yeah, but not in the way you are thinking, Taylor thought.

"But! The enemy knows no fear! It will rarely stop to take cover or be intimidated by anything you throw at it. And when they are bearing down on you and your magazine runs dry and worse still, you're out of ammo, what do you do?"

"Run!" one replied as the others laughed in response.

"You'd like to, wouldn't you? And every part of your brain should be telling you to do so. You'd have to be crazy, absolutely insane to stand your ground, or, a marine!"

Several nearby the student who had cried out slapped him as he cowered down in shame, and others laughed at him. It was a stage, and he was pandering to a crowd.

How did I ever get this job?

He put down the rifle and picked up an Assegai.

"A stick! Run!" one of them yelled.

"That's an Assegai, idiot!" another replied.

Good, they're starting to learn.

"When you're up close and personal with a Mech, you'll be glad of one of these."

He powered it up and stepped over to the Mech that was still smouldering from the rounds he had put through it. With his other hand, he knocked on the armour. It barely echoed at all and emitted a low drone showing just how substantial it was. He held up the Assegai for all to behold, and then thrust it forward into the Mech armour.

It drove through with little resistance and ran up to the hilt. He ripped it back out, and a blue liquid spewed out with the weapon.

He knew it wasn't real alien blood, but the crowd didn't, and they loved the spectacle. He carried on talking for another twenty minutes, with Jafar standing beside him, looking thoroughly dismayed and bored while he talked them through what it was to be a marine and face the enemy they had come to know so well. Finally, it was coming to a close, and Jafar's moment to join the spectacle. Taylor picked up a shield and an unpowered training Assegai before turning back to his audience.

"The Mech enemy is big, powerful, and stronger than any human. But through the innovation of Reitech Industries, we've evened up the score. With this equipment, we can move faster, hit harder, and take more punishment. Even so, we must use our biggest assets to our advantage, speed, agility, and raw willpower. The enemy may have changed, but the essence of what is important to being a marine has always remained the same!"

He pointed towards Jafar and beckoned for his mock enemy to come forward. He taunted the alien, which excited the crowd further.

"Come on, you big metal bastard!" he yelled.

Jafar suddenly moved from his statue-like position he had held since coming on stage. He took a fighting stance and approached Taylor. They both knew a Mech would have a gun in hand, but that wasn't what Weaver wanted in his display. Jafar took up an almost boxing style of pose. It was familiar to the audience and provided plenty of entertainment. Taylor could hardly be enthusiastic about it, but he knew Jafar would at least punish him if he were lazy. He lifted his shield and circled his opponent with caution.

Jafar leapt forward with just a little more speed than a Mech really would. He was supposed to try and simulate the speed, agility, and intelligence of a typical alien warrior, but clearly he had either forgotten, or more likely wanted a bit of a challenge. Taylor lifted his shield, and the brunt of the blow impacted on it before sliding off. Taylor spun off to the side to avoid being crushed by the seemingly charging bull.

The crowd were quiet as they watched in amazement. Taylor rushed forward with his shield held before him, but Jafar grabbed it with both hands and launched him into the air. Taylor made a wild swing with his weapon, but he was already being projected through the air and missed by a long shot. He landed hard and rolled across the floor. Jafar threw down the shield in mock distain that further enthralled the crowd. They booed as if watching a wrestling match.

Taylor knew otherwise. Jafar was his friend, but that didn't mean he was going to go easy on him. He got to his feet and rushed at Jafar, appearing to be doing so through rage. But as Jafar swung for him with the clumsy heavy arms of the Mech suit, he ducked under and rolled. Back on his feet, he evaded a back fist swing and thrust the Assegai up into the Mech chest armour. The electrified tip sent a quick pulse of energy through the suit, causing it to spasm before shutting down.

The crowd cheered in sheer ecstasy, and a hail of comments hurled forward in praise of the Colonel. He sighed in relief as Jafar smiled back at him from the immobilised suit.

"Almost had me there," he jested.

"You're slowing down."

"Yeah, thanks."

Taylor lifted his leg and kicked the centre of the Mech suit. It toppled over onto its back and landed with a satisfying crash to once and for all show defeat. The crowd loved it, and he knew that scene alone would ensure recruitment of many of the young men and women there. It made him feel a little sick, for they were presenting war with the Mechs as an adventure, which it never had been for any of them.

Never mind, maybe they'll never have to face the invaders.

But he knew in his heart that it would not be so.

"Well, well, what a great display from our very own hero, Colonel Mitch Taylor!" yelled Weaver, as he got up from his seat and approached the stage between the centre of the audience. They fell silent and looked at the civilian clothed man in a suit with suspicion.

"Let's see him kick some more ass!" one of them yelled.

Several others hollered in agreement.

"Taylor, Taylor, Taylor!" they began to shout and stamp their feet.

Weaver leapt onto the stage with a huge grin on his face and lifted his arms up to call for silence. He didn't get it. Turning to Taylor, he asked for assistance. It pleased the Colonel to know who held the power. He lifted up his palm, and the room instantly went still.

"You've heard from one of our country's great heroes, and you've seen the weapons our brave Marine Corps use. You've even seen a friendly demonstration of them in use, but what would you say to see those skills and weapons being put to the test against a living and breathing enemy? How would you like to see it done for real?"

They went wild with excitement, as Weaver turned back to Taylor with a smirk.

"What are you doing?" Taylor asked. He was suspicious of the man.

"Only giving the people what they want."

"You're a real fucking humanitarian."

"What's the matter, afraid of a little danger?"

"In your dreams. You can try your metal against me any time, and the result will always be the same."

"Not me, Colonel. One of them."

He lifted a small remote controller and pressed a

button. The divider at the back of the stage split and slid open. Taylor was appalled to see a Mech. A huge hydraulic column restrained it, and he could already see where this was going.

"You're not serious? Have you lost your mind?"

The crowd died down as they watched and waited. Taylor paced over to Weaver because he could no longer talk across the stage without everyone in the room hearing.

"This is insane. You've brought a live Mech warrior here?"

"It's not armed."

"Armed? Christ, you're a fucking idiot! Millions fought and died fighting those bastards so those at home would never have to see them," he whispered.

"And neither do they have to. But look at these fine men and women, the future of the Corps. They want to follow in the valiant footsteps of Colonel Taylor, the legend," he replied with a sleazy smile. "Now, you can either play along with this and do what you are trained and paid to do, or suffer the humiliation that you are simply too scared. We made you the nation's hero, and we can take it away just as easily."

Taylor shook his head. He couldn't believe what he was hearing, but he looked out to his enthusiastic audience and knew he had no choice.

"Can't believe you sprung this shit on me in the middle of a talk," he muttered.

"Maybe if you ever turned up for the discussion on these matters, you might be better informed."

He knew that was bullshit because he'd never have agreed to it had it been mentioned to him.

I wonder if Weaver is pushing for an audience response or just trying to make me suffer, but it doesn't matter now.

"Goddamn you, Weaver."

He paced past to address the eager crowd.

"So here is the real deal, a Mech, one of their very own who was sent to this world to destroy the human race. You might have heard of the exploits of 2nd Inter-Allied and how we dealt with these monsters, but now it's time to see it firsthand!"

He stepped towards the rifle; the clip had been removed. He looked up to Weaver to see him holding it.

"Not like that, Colonel. They want a spectacle," he replied, gesturing towards the live Assegai he had so recently used to show its penetration against the Mech armour.

Doesn't get any better, he thought to himself.

As he stepped over and took up the weapon, he noticed Jafar getting to his feet, having recovered from the energy pulse sent through his armour.

"You hear what he wants?" Taylor asked him.

"Yes."

"Crazy."

Jafar grunted casually, as if he didn't agree.

"What, you think this is smart?"

"Your skills haven't been tested in years."

"You don't think I've done enough to prove my ability?"

"Yes, but now you must maintain that reputation, and be ready for when you need to use those skills again."

"So there is no end to the fighting? War is over, but we have to keep fighting to be ready for the next one?"

Jafar nodded in agreement.

"Great."

Weaver continued playing to the crowd. "Let's hear it for the great Colonel Taylor as he takes on a Mech single-handed in a no rules, no holes barred fight to the death!"

The excitement that ensued was electrifying. Taylor wasn't scared of having to fight, but it seemed futile and stupid to risk his life for a little entertainment, and he could not help but feel it made light of the danger posed by the Mechs.

These aren't to be toyed with.

With a faked enthusiasm, he paced over and lifted his shield from the ground where it had lain since Jafar launched him through the air. As he knelt down, he felt his knee give way slightly and his flank go rigid. He must have landed harder than he had realised. He sucked it up and hid the impediment. Looking back to his audience, he lifted the shield and Assegai as a crowd pleaser that spurred them on further. He turned back to his opponent.

"Don't fuck this up now," whispered Weaver, as he

strolled passed with an even more despicable sleazy grin than usual.

"Not him you gotta worry about. It's me after this is over. Should never have been allowed."

"We'll see," he said and turned to the crowd after passing beyond the barriers. Only Jafar remained inside with the two of them, and he was unarmed just as the Mech was.

"Ladies and Gentlemen, let the battle begin!" Weaver shouted.

He lifted a controller and pressed a button; the restraints on the Mech released. He leaned in against the barrier and glared at Jafar.

"It's Taylor's fight now. Not a move."

Jafar grunted, and they both knew he wouldn't listen to the command.

The enemy Mech looked up and around the stage suspiciously, as if expecting a trap of some kind. It was right to be suspicious. The whole situation was ridiculous, but Taylor was powerless to stop it except through vanquishing his foe. The creature's attention turned to him once it was satisfied there was not a trick afoot. It leapt into action and rushed Taylor like a raging bull. He narrowly avoided the beast by turning off to one side. It came at him again, and as he lifted his shield and stepped off to his right side, he felt his knee weaken, and he couldn't move quickly enough. The huge Mech thundered into his shield and launched him off his feet. Taylor hit the clear shielding around what had become their cage and slumped down to the floor.

His head ached, but the helmet had saved him from any major injury. Jafar lifted himself as if to intervene, but Weaver hit another control that cut all power to his suit and locked him inside like a statue. He looked over to Weaver with a piercing glare they both knew had deadly intent behind it.

"I told you not to get involved. You forget who runs this show," he stated while looking exceptionally happy with himself.

"Get up!" Jafar shouted to Taylor.

He was powerless to act and that only made him more furious.

"Get up!" he roared again. The Mech was advancing towards Taylor.

The Mech reached him and lifted its right leg to stamp down on the Colonel. He regained composure just in time to see the foot that would bring instant death looming over him. He quickly swung the shield at its other leg and hit with all his force. The swipe of the heavy shield smashed the creature's planted leg and took it off balance, causing it to crash to the ground and onto its back. It was barely enough time for him to get his senses back and clamber to his feet.

Taylor ached all over from the impact, but his knee

seemed to be working right again, and he shook off the pain and drowsiness. He looked over to see Jafar was frozen solid. He gazed at the audience. Several were filming it with handheld devices.

Shit!

He looked back to Jafar. "You gonna help?"

"He can't help you, Taylor," Weaver said. He lifted his controller and smiled.

"What's the problem?" asked Jafar. "You've killed far greater enemies."

Taylor nodded in agreement, but his body didn't seem to agree. Years of living in peace, and being given light base duties as a result of his status, had softened his abilities more than he realised, but there was no time to fret over it. The audience was silent now and waiting with baited breath to see a conclusion to the fight. He knew he had to give them more than a victory. He needed to give them a spectacular display.

"All right, you son of a bitch," he whispered to himself.

He raced towards the creature. As it swung for him, he ducked under and drove his Assegai up into its torso, but he did not stop there. Blue blood spewed out as he reclaimed his blade and spun around striking the Mech with his shield. It staggered back, and the crowd cheered as a trail of blood coated the floor. It came at him once more with a huge hammer blow that he voided and used the power of his suit to leap into the air. His legs went up over, and he somersaulted around onto its shoulders.

The Mech tried desperately to reach up and grab hold of him, but it was too late. He drove his Assegai down into its faceplate, and the beast immediately went limp. The body crashed down face first to the floor and delivered Taylor back onto his feet. A pool of blood expanded out from the wound where the Assegai was still impeded and left for sheer effect.

The audience was speechless for a few seconds, as they saw the blue blood engulf the soles of the Colonel's boots. He finally threw up his shield triumphantly, and it was all they needed to go wild. Wolf whistles and applause echoed throughout the room. Even Weaver looked pleased.

"Thought you wanted to see me lose?"

"Oh, no, seeing you bleed a little is enough for me," he said, looking at the small trickle of blood coming from the Colonel's mouth. "Far from it, this has been an immense success and speaks volumes of the potential of such displays in the future."

"We ain't doing this again," he snapped back.

"Why on earth not? Look at them," he said, gesturing towards the ecstatic mob. "Not man enough?"

"Not stupid enough. I fought that war because I had to, not for fun or entertainment."

"Wrong again, Colonel. You fought because you were told to and because you were paid to. Just as you will continue to do whatever is ordered and required of you now."

"Yeah, well, we'll see about that, won't we?"

"What are you gonna do? Leave? Go and take some shitty 9-5 dead end job where you know no one and nobody cares for you. And you won't be taking your friend here along. He's a soldier till the day he dies."

"Marine."

"What was that?"

"Marine, you asshole."

"Colonel, don't know if you looked recently, but he ain't one of us, never will be. He's an asset, a fighter when we need him to be, and a circus act when we don't. He knows his place. Maybe you should, too."

Weaver turned back to his audience with a grandiose smile across his face and throwing his arms up in the air, as if it was he who had been victorious.

"Well, how about that!" he yelled. "You've played the video games, you've watched the movies, but have you ever seen it done for real? The real deal, the real steel; a marine taking on one of the enemy's deadliest warriors in close combat and winning. Let me hear it for the Colonel!"

It was sounding more and more like a boxing match analysis, and he didn't appreciate it at all. He stepped past the screens as they slid back and around Weaver to address the audience personally.

"There it is. They aren't pretty, and fighting them is no joke. I pray none of you ever have to, but it's my job to make sure that if you join the Corps, you are fully prepared to do just that. Thank you for your time and good luck."

He dropped his shield to the ground and paced off, leaving his Assegai still firmly impeded in his vanquished foe. He stopped for a moment beside his friend to see he was still immobile. He shot a murderous glance at Weaver, who gave in and clicked a button on his remote that reactivated the suit. The two of them carried on in disgust.

"You aren't wearing that piece of crap again," he snarled.

CHAPTER TWO

They raced through the warm Arizona night in Taylor's own open top jeep. Jafar's head stuck out over the windscreen and into the path of the wind, but he didn't care.

"That was a mockery of all we ever achieved and fought for," stated Taylor.

He got no response.

"What, you have no opinion?"

"Surprised you thought it would go any other way," he finally replied.

"What, turning humanity's greatest struggle for survival into a theatre act?"

"Is that not what peace is?"

It silenced Taylor as he thought more on it.

"I didn't see so many friends die for us to reach this point."

"This is your purpose now."

"So we just carry on doing this?"

"Until another opportunity presents itself. I am at the will of your commanders as much as you are. Until the next war comes, we must weather it."

"You really look forward to the next war that much?"

"Is it so surprising when looking at the alternative lives we now lead?"

It was true that Taylor missed the companionship of his troops he had enjoyed during the wars, but it seemed a monumental price to pay for those few moments of friendship.

"Where are we going?" asked Jafar.

"To find a bar, nothing else to do."

A few kilometres down the road they came across a secluded establishment that would be all but hidden from view on the sparse desert road, were it not for the neon lights garishly illuminating the sight for all passersby. They said nothing more than 'bar', with no indication of a name.

"Is is wise to enter a local establishment after the last occasion?" asked Jafar.

"I don't give a shit, and anyway, so what if we get into trouble? You enjoy it."

Jafar shrugged his shoulders, unable to disagree. The jeep rolled to a halt in the open plain next to the building that vaguely resembled a parking lot. It was relatively busy considering the remote location.

Taylor strode to the door and smashed it open to find

a number of patrons staring at him. He still had on his fatigues from the demonstration earlier. The only rank identification was well worn and barely visible from where it had rubbed on the Reitech armour. They seemed relatively inviting for a second, and then Jafar stepped through into the room behind him. The tall and broad alien had to duck down to get through the door, and his presence made them all freeze and stare with their jaws almost hitting the floor.

All conversations in the room stopped; the only sound emanating from a jukebox at the side of the room with some old rock music of the kind Taylor appreciated.

"Looks like my kind of place," he stated.

There was no response until the two of them took a step further in, and the barkeep finally spoke out.

"Hang on, son, what are you doing bringing one of them in here? This some kind of joke?"

A few of the patrons grunted in approval of the words.

"Wait, that's Taylor, ain't it?" whispered one of them.

He looked over to see but didn't recognise the man.

Great, another asshole who wants to make a point, he thought.

"Yeah, that's Colonel Taylor!"

The others looked at him with a little less suspicion and were starting to come around, realising a TV personality was among them.

Nothing like a bit of star power.

He didn't want their praise, their gratitude, or even to

be recognised.

"Just here for a drink."

"Well, you sure can come in...but...err not with your friend there," said the barkeep.

Taylor shook his head. He wasn't surprised; it had happened enough times it was becoming boring.

"All right, now you listen up. I bet there's more than a few of you here who fought in the war, but I can guarantee you that my friend here killed more of those bastards than all of you put together, and then some!"

There was no response.

"We both gave everything to protect this country and this planet, so I don't want to hear any bitchin' about where we can and can't buy a beer. We're staying, and anyone who has something to say about it, they better do so now!"

Several looked away, and it was clear that despite many not being happy about it, they were not going to speak up.

"That's what I thought," he said loudly.

He strolled to the bar confidently and defiantly with Jafar by his side. Half of the patrons watched their every move, while the others turned away and tried to ignore their presence. It made Taylor wonder what on Earth they were fighting for if they were going to be seen as such outcasts.

"Two beers," he said to the barkeep.

The man now had little choice. He passed over two

bottles and sighed as he took Taylor's money. A few seconds later, he was squirreling off, pretending to be busy with other customers when it was clear he only intended to gossip. Taylor rested back against the bar edge and swilled his beer.

In just a few seconds, they had gone from the centre of attention to being almost invisible. Conversations continued all around them. He felt as if they had vanished beyond sight or sound.

"Nice to feel wanted," he muttered.

"You always seem to want appreciation for your efforts, why?" Jafar asked.

"Maybe because we fucking deserve it. Look at what we achieved in the wars, and now half the World or more treats us like shit. Easy to forget our efforts when there isn't an occupation force around the corner."

Jafar seemed to have nothing more to say on the subject.

"Oh, come on, you want to say something, so say it."

"We are for war. It is our purpose."

"And?"

"We need another."

Taylor sighed as he thought about the prospect. One of his biggest fears of another war was that it would take him away from Parker, and yet he seemed to see her less and less since they had won the war.

"All the people you hold dear coming together to do what they were born and bred to do."

"And die as well?"

"We all die eventually."

He was starting to understand how the aliens could fight so fearlessly in combat. He hated to admit it, but he was beginning to miss the war. Not the death or loss of friends, but the companionship, the sense of purpose.

Now where am I? Surrounded by a group of assholes who'd rather have me thrown out the door than make conversation.

In the background something caught his eye, and he turned to see his name along the top of a video game machine at the side of the room. The board above it read 'Battle Ops 2: Taylor's Triumph'. There was a picture of a soldier loosely resembling him on a poster at the side holding an American flag up in the air.

"What the hell is that?" he whispered.

Jafar had overheard and turned to see the same. He could see the image of Taylor and noticed a dead Mech under one of the character's boot. He chuckled a little, but Taylor did not seem amused. He pushed off from the bar where he had been leaning and strolled over to the machine. A preview video ran on it, showing the first person action shooter it was.

As he approached, a young man took up position at the controls. He pulled on a virtual reality headset and took up a gun-like object from the machine. The man must have been no more than nineteen, and Taylor would more aptly call him a boy. He started moving all of a sudden, walking on the spot. He was standing on a three hundred and sixty degree treadmill. Clearly, the screen Taylor was watching was merely to draw people in and audiences to watch, as the boy was completely immersed in the game.

Taylor could do nothing for a few minutes as he stood in astonishment at what he was seeing. The lad playing was running through corridors, gunning down Mechs left right and centre. His Assegai flashed out occasionally, as the in game character rolled across the floor and thrust it into an enemy soldier or leapt up athletically onto the back of another in an effortless manner of which he could only dream of.

"You see, you like war. Everyone does," stated Jafar.

He was surprised at the voice, for he had not even noticed his friend approach his side. They continued to watch for a few minutes in amazement. Taylor seemed a one-man army in the game, supported by only a few comrades who did little but seemingly elevate his epic abilities. As a level came to a close, the lad came up against a huge Mech villain, the likes of which Taylor had never seen. It was five times the size of any enemy soldier, like some giant war machine.

"Not seen anything like that before."

"No, but something similar on some worlds," replied Jafar.

Another terror we are yet to face, he thought.

"How the hell do they know about them, then?"

He already knew the answer before he had finished asking it, artistic licence.

The lad playing was frantically lashing out at the huge in game creature but was struck and grasped by its huge mechanical claws. The body of Taylor on screen was lifted and snapped at the spine before being tossed to the floor, and the letters 'game over' appearing in large letters.

"Goddamn it!" yelled the boy.

The scene took Taylor aback. It was a visceral and eye-opening reminder of what could, or might still be his fate. He often wondered how he had survived through so many deadly situations. As the boy took off the mask, he recoiled in shock at Taylor and his huge friend looming over and staring at the console.

"What the fuck?" he screamed.

Several in the room went silent as they looked over to the two strangers and sought reason to cause trouble.

"It's okay, kid, just watching," Taylor said, snapping out of it.

The teenager was still in shock and had clearly not been in the room or noticed when they had arrived. He first looked in absolute fear at Jafar, and then to Taylor. His expression changed to a smile when he realised who they were.

"No fucking way."

Taylor didn't respond. He was still shocked at the game that seemed to trivialise everything they had worked to achieve, and even the deaths of those around him.

"No fucking way, it's really you, and with your alien turncoat!"

Taylor's face turned to a grimace, taking offence at the word. He wanted to strike the teenager for it but restrained himself, realising where he was and who stood before him. He felt his skin boil in anger, but thinking of what Chandra would have done in such circumstances made him rise above it.

"So fucking cool to meet you!" yelled the teenager. "You're one sick motherfucker."

He didn't know how to respond, but the boy gave him little opportunity.

"You must have killed hundreds of Krys, man?"

He'd not heard the abbreviation before, but it didn't take a whole lot of imagination to work it out. The lad tapped him on the chest as he continued on in a manner he did not appreciate.

"So come on, my man, how many you kill?"

"Enough," he replied.

"Oh, come on, you fucked 'em up proper good. Tell me what it's like."

Visions flashed through his mind of the seemingly endless bloodshed he had witnessed. The gruesome scenes of genocide from where they had rescued Jones stuck with him the most. But what harrowed him even more was the fact he had not been there for two of his closest friends when they met their end, Friday and Chandra. When it came down to it, he could not be there and could not save those he cared for most. Jones and Parker had barely made it through. That was what he could see, not those who had died at his hands.

"Come on, tell me. You must have fucking slaughtered them!"

He tapped Taylor again, and he had heard enough. His arm snapped up and took the lad's in a firm hold; enough to freeze him in place but not harm him. He tried to struggle, but it was no good.

"You trivialise war. You mock all those who fought and died, so you can play these shitty videogames. What kind of a man are you?"

The lad was stunned and froze. His face was going white, and it was evidently the most fear he had ever experienced. That only made Taylor angrier.

"Remember the wars. Honour those who served in them, but do not make light of their sacrifices. A day may come when your generation has to take on the job, and you will find it a very different experience."

His jaw dropped, and he tried to get out words but couldn't for a few seconds until he finally gasped for air and opened up.

"I am sorry, fucking sorry, man. I didn't mean it. I love you guys."

A coarse voice sounded off to their side that brought

silence to those around them.

"You done kissing ass, kid, or you wanna get a room with this soldier boy?"

Taylor turned to see the comment had come from a tall man who was almost as wide as he was high. He wore a close fitting vest that only served to make him look like a slob. Despite this, he had arms as thick as tree trunks. Maybe he couldn't run a marathon, but he wasn't a man to be tussled with. He turned his attention to Taylor as he swilled his beer and licked his chops. His head was bold and reflected the light from the ceiling lamps. A large gold chain hung around his neck, and one of his ears was pierced with a large hoop. His face was stubbled and red cheeked. Bags sat under his eyes from a man who had spent half his life drinking.

"What do ya say, soldier boy? Why don't you head on and find a bent bar to get your end away? And take your alien freak here with you."

"You sound like a man of some experience," Taylor replied dryly.

The response both confused and angered the man, for the humour went over his head, but that only served to entertain those watching a little more. The youngster stepped between them to address the huge fat thug.

"Hey come on, man. This is Taylor. He's a legend."

"Yeah, this piece of shit? Not here, he ain't. Get out of now before you get fucked up."

He shoved the lad and sent him flying with little effort. He crashed over a chair and hit the ground hard. Taylor knelt down and hauled him to his feet.

"Stay out of this, son. You'll only get hurt."

He turned back to the greasy thug. He looked him up and down for a second. He seemed twice the man Taylor was, in weight at least.

"What are you looking at?" he sneered.

The entire bar had now silenced and turned their attention to the standoff.

"A sack of shit who's wasting my time," he replied quickly.

A few of the man's friends took a few paces closer to have his back as they could see it was about to kick off. Jafar did the same, but Taylor lifted his hand to tell him to stop.

"I got this."

"Oh, you got this, have you?" asked the thug. "Only thing you got is an ass whooping coming. I don't like soldier boys."

"Marine, asshole!"

The man had heard enough and lifted his beer bottle which he had reversed while they spoke, so he now held it by the neck. It was a clumsy move, and one Taylor had fully anticipated. He kicked forward hard into the man's belly. It did little to move the hulking mass but enough to throw him off balance. He stumbled back into his friends who caught him and barely managed to hold his weight up. They threw him back towards Taylor, and he came out swinging with the biggest hook Taylor had ever seen.

He knew the weight would be too much to stop, so he ducked under and drove his knee up into the man's huge bulking stomach. The air was pushed out of him. He folded over the Colonel's strike and went limp for a second. Taylor grabbed the top of his vest and yanked him upright and punched him hard in the face, which threw him back to his friends once again.

"Why don't you quit before you really feel some pain?"

The man spat out blood on the floor in front of Taylor and looked furious. It was clear to everyone that he wasn't going to let it stand. He grabbed the nearest bottle and smashed it on the table beside him, holding it up ready to use. Taylor smiled as the fool held it before him rather than back and out of the way. He rushed forward with surprising speed and thrust with the sharpened glass. Taylor pushed down with both hands over the bottle and onto the man's wrist and gripped hard. He stepped under his armpit and thrust his body up so that he almost dislocated the arm. The man squirmed in agony. The bottle dropped from his grasp and smashed on the hard floor in front of them.

Taylor twisted back out from under the man's arm and struck where his ribs would be with several punches, though his first met nothing but fat. Seeing it was having little effect, he leapt forward with a knee that smashed the man back. As the two of them stumbled across the room under the power of Taylor's attack, one of the thug's friends lifted a chair and swung for Taylor. He tried to duck under, but his forward momentum made it impossible. He lifted his hands just in time to have the chair crash over his body and splinter into a hundred parts.

Pain soared through Taylor's arm. He felt wood splinters pierce his flesh, but there was no time to check it. He was down on one knee from the impact, and the man was already bearing down on him with one of the legs from the chair. He jumped up and threw his arm up to parry the strike at the forearm where there was the least power. The man head-butted him in response, but it did little except make him angrier. He jammed his thumb into his attacker's wrist at the pressure point, causing him to give him the leg.

Now armed with an improvised truncheon, Taylor was ready to go to work. He smashed it across his attacker's cheek and watched the man tumble over to the floor. As he did, he was tackled by another and hit the floor hard. His head impacted, and the shock made him blackout for just a few seconds. His eyes opened to see a fist coming towards his face and pushed him back into the floor. He reached over for the table leg and smashed it across the man's face, throwing him off to the side.

Taylor tilted his head back while still on the floor and saw Jafar standing about idle and watching the display.

"Not gonna help?"

"You said not to."

"When did I say that?"

He looked up to see a foot about to slam into his face. He quickly rolled over, clambered to his feet, and looked over to Jafar again.

"You want help now?" asked his friend.

"Yes!" Taylor hollered.

The hulking thug was now on his feet and once more coming at Taylor. He swung clumsily again. This time Taylor parried the strike with his left, and with his right grabbed hold of the huge hoop in the thug's ear and ripped it way through the flesh of his lobe.

With a big hook, Taylor smashed the man to the ground as he cupped his ear in agony. But a few seconds later, his pained expression turned to anger, and he was coming at him like a raging bull. Taylor had no time to move and did his best to brace for impact, but from his flank came Jafar at lighting speed. He barged the huge man aside, throwing him onto a nearby table that collapsed under his weight. His friends stopped for a moment at the scene, turning their attention back to Taylor and his alien friend.

"Get 'em!" one yelled.

Six men rushed at them brandishing chairs and bottles. The bar erupted into a hail of punches and bloodshed. Five minutes later, Taylor and Jafar stood over the bodies of their attackers who were now unconscious or incapacitated in some way. The rest of the bar's patrons could do nothing but watch in amazement. Blood poured from Taylor's nose where he had been struck more than a few times, and his jaw ached like hell. Despite the pain, he managed to break a smile to Jafar.

Sirens could be heard approaching on the road outside, but they made no attempt to run.

"You're going down for this!" shouted the barkeep.

He rushed out from behind the bar with a scattergun in hand as if to act all tough, now he knew he had the authorities close to hand.

The young lad who Taylor had so recently been conversing with leapt forward to jump in the way.

"Hey, come on, you saw who started this!"

"You keep your mouth shut, kid! These boys came in here looking for trouble, and they found it." He turned his attention to Taylor again, "We don't want your kind here. You fucking soldier boys are all the same. No war to fight, so you start one."

"Marine," replied Taylor sharply.

"What?"

The barkeep rushed up to Taylor with his gun and tried to jam it in his face.

"What was that you said?"

Taylor gave him not a second longer to make his pathetic attempt at intimidation. He snatched the barrel of the gun and ripped it from the man's arms and turned it on him.

"I didn't spend years of fighting and losing friends to put up with this shit."

He spun the stock around and struck the man's face, breaking his nose. He dropped to his knees, blood pouring through his hands as they cupped his bleeding face.

The door of the bar burst open and police rushed in. Taylor instantly released his grip, as to not be gunned down by trigger-happy local authorities, but he was still as calm as ever.

"You just remember who it was who fought so you could live your life," he stated.

He knew his words would be lost on the bar owner, but he seemed to get some sympathy from those watching. Others were disgusted by his actions and seemed to view him as the sort of degenerate who they'd rather have behind bars.

"Freeze!"

It was over. Six cops all ready to pull the trigger rushed them. Two pushed Taylor over against the wall to cuff him. They tried the same to Jafar but could not move him. One stuffed a gun in his face and screamed. "Turn around! You are under arrest!"

He looked to Taylor first. He wouldn't take the command from a stranger. Taylor nodded in agreement for his friend to accept their fate, but he smiled at the cops, revealing blood seeping into the gaps of his teeth.

In response, one drew a shock baton and drove it into his stomach. His went limp and dropped to his knees.

"Not so funny now, is it?" the cop shouted in his ear.

* * *

The night seemed to have gone on forever as Taylor sat on a hard bench in a prison cell. After what he'd been through in military detention, it didn't seem so bad. Jafar sat in a cell opposite him. He was willing to bet good money that his alien friend would be capable of prising the bars apart with his bare hands, but he had done as ordered and gone along with it. Hours had passed without a word between the two of them when Jafar finally spoke out.

"Yesterday you tried to get out of a fight any way possible, and yet in the night, you sought one, why?"

It gave Taylor pause for thought.

"You say you don't want to fight anymore, but then enjoy it when the time comes."

"A good honest bar brawl is the end to a good evening. Fighting a war is something I would wish on no man."

He wasn't sure he necessarily believed that whole-heartedly, but it seemed like the best way of explaining it.

"But you were asked to fight a war, just one Mech. An unarmed Mech. How is that different to what we just did?"

He didn't have an answer. Somehow in his head it made sense, and he had enjoyed every minute of the brawl, and hated the Mech fight and the reasons for it.

"Your people only seem to like and respect you when there is a war and when you are fighting it, and yet you wish for peace?"

The questions were getting more trying and piercing Taylor's thoughts.

Yes, maybe I do pray for another war.

A door opened at the far end of the corridor dividing their two cells, and they could hear three pairs of footsteps approaching. Neither of them got up to greet their visitors. Two cops and Weaver came into view. Weaver was shaking his head in disgust and disapproval.

"You're a maniac who should be locked away in times of peace for the good of society. But someone, somewhere thinks you have a part to play. You're a relic, Taylor, one that will be paraded around until nobody longer cares and then thrown aside. I can just see your life ten years from now. Sitting in a trailer park somewhere, alone and drinking yourself to death. Replaying the glory days in your head while nobody gives a shit anymore."

Taylor wanted nothing more than to reach through the bars of the cell and throttle the detestable creature. He only restrained himself because the only thing he wanted more was to get out of the cell.

"And a good morning to you," he replied sarcastically.

Weaver shook his head. He was clearly trying to get a rise out of Mitch and give them all an excuse to keep him behind bars, but he wasn't biting.

"Let him out."

"Bail ain't even been paid," protested one of he officers, "This guy wrecked a whole bar and half the patrons in it."

"I think that's exaggerating. He's one man, not an army. Now, you know who I work for. Let him out before I have to start making calls you don't want me to make. And let that thing out while you're at it," Weaver said, waving towards Jafar.

The cop reluctantly swiped his security card through the cell access point, and the door slid open.

"There's a first time for everything," said Taylor.

"How so?" Weaver asked.

"I'm happy to see you," he sneered.

"All right, let's go."

The two of them followed Weaver out of the cellblock to the front of the station where they heard cheering coming from the front desk. They got to the atrium to see two police officers watching a video of his fight with the Mech the previous day. It had clearly been filmed by one of the audience. He could see the crowd come into view on the edges.

"That you?" asked one of them.

"Fucking epic," added one of the others.

"Yes," added Weaver. "That little stunt of ours has caused quite a stir since it has gone viral; five million views in less than a day. A lot of people can see plenty of potential in that."

"In what? Live assassinations? We used to condemn and invade countries for it."

"Times change, as you should learn. The people want what they want, and I'll happily give it to them."

"As long as it doesn't risk your own neck."

"Precisely, Taylor."

Taylor didn't like what he was hearing, and he doubted he'd like what was coming in the next few weeks even less, but right now, he was just relieved to be free once more.

"You have a driver waiting out front. He'll take you directly to the Deveron where you'll be transported back to base. You've got a few days leave, anyway. When you come back, you can be guaranteed we'll have something to keep you on your toes."

What an asshole! Taylor thought, walking off in disgust.

CHAPTER THREE

It was close to evening when Taylor finally got to his home on base. As he approached the door with his key card in hand, it slid open. Parker stood at the entrance to greet him. She no longer wore the uniform of a marine. She was dressed as a private contractor in military style but non-unit specific gear fatigues. She looked curious for a moment at the bruising on his face.

"Should I ask?"

"Probably not," he took her in a firm embrace and lifted her off her feet as he carried on through the doorway.

"So how's life treating you in the private sector?"

"Can't complain about the pay. Few more years of this, and we can live wherever we please."

He seemed surprised.

"You think I should follow after you? I thought you loved the Corps?"

"But I love you more, and if I can't have both, then you know what I'll choose."

He sat down wearily on the sofa, and she sympathetically grabbed a beer for him.

"Come on, let's not make it about this again. You know I'd have stayed if there was any way."

Taylor knew it to be true. Since the war was over, there was little chance of them getting away with their relationship any longer with the way things stood. But half the time it felt like he'd lost another comrade-in-arms.

"Looks like you gave more than a talk out there."

He smiled in response.

"Just some idiots at a bar."

"You keep doing that and you're gonna be in some real trouble."

"Really? What are they gonna do? They need me."

"For now, but you're not going to be young forever."

"Yeah, thanks."

Weaver had threatened his existence in a similar manner, but coming from someone he loved gave him pause for concern. Fatigue was setting in and the realisation that he really hadn't had much sleep. He knew his body would appreciate the rest, for it was bruised and battered. It wasn't long before he was out for the count.

As the sun rose, he woke to find Parker beside him. It brought a smile to his face. That smile was lost as he noticed a flashing light on the comms screen on the wall, an incoming message.

Can't be from anyone I want to hear from, he thought.

He started to move which got protests from Parker as she groaned and tried to keep him put.

"I gotta take this."

"Right now? You're on leave."

"Yeah, but I already caused enough trouble lately. Let's not invite more."

"Mmm," she finally agreed.

He stepped up to the console and tapped it for the message to begin. He'd expected video, but there was only text. It was from General White's personal aide with orders from his superior. It simply read 'Report to General White as soon as you read this'. It was an ominous message of the sort he'd not expect from the General.

"What is it?" asked Eli.

"Looks like leave is cancelled."

"What? You only just got here," she protested.

"Tell me about it."

She crawled out of bed and stood behind him with her arms over his shoulders.

"You must plead your case to the General. You've done enough."

He turned around in surprise.

"Out of the Corps, and already you're no longer thinking like a marine. We don't bargain with our superiors. If we are called upon, we are there one hundred percent. How would we have won this war if marines chose whether to report for duty?"

She shook her head. "But we're not at war, are we? You can't keep doing this. All we did during the war was look forward to a life together and away from it all, but where are we now? Worse off than ever."

He had no answer for her because he felt the same.

Maybe it's time to give it all up.

He'd never admit it though. He didn't rush to respond to the message. An hour later, he presented himself for the General. White was close to retirement now, and Taylor didn't look forward to the day he was replaced.

As he walked into the room, he could smell a mix of furniture polish and whiskey. He entered with a smile, but it was removed when he could see the expression on White's face. He had the look of a man who to give someone bad news and hated having to do it.

"Morning, Sir," said Taylor.

He smiled in response but did not speak, gesturing for Taylor to come in casually and sit before him.

"Now I know you were due some R&R, Mitch, and I can't think of a man more deserving, but these orders come from above my head.

"Spit it out, Sir."

"Your fight with that Mech the other day has caused quite a stir. I can't say I liked the idea, and I can assure you I had no part to play in it. However, we cannot shy away from the fact it is now a global phenomenon. The video has gone viral, and they love it."

"And why should we care?"

"Your work now is to publicise the Corps and provide a positive recruiting role model for the next generation. So we may not like it, but you just single-handedly won over millions of people in a couple of minutes, doing nothing more than you were trained to do and have been doing for years."

"You don't really want to keep that circus going?"

"If the method works, then I can live with a lot. You remember what it was like after the last war ended. Nobody wanted to know about the Corps or signing up for future conflicts. This has struck home and is getting people thinking about it on a daily basis. This is exactly what we need to get some damn enthusiasm. Hell, almost nobody wants to sign up anymore. We lost massive numbers in the wars, and as many again who retired or found some other path out. Do you know how many thousands of marines we have lost to PTSD and who will never return to duty?"

"I think I know better than most," Taylor replied sharply.

The General sighed in response. He didn't like locking horns with Taylor. Neither of them wanted to be discussing the subject, and yet they knew it was their duty to do so.

"So whoever is running this, what do they want from me?"

"Another fight."

He knew it would be the answer, but he still gasped.

"Haven't I fought enough for this country...this planet?"

"And that is why they want you, in France. A guaranteed safe bet. They want someone who can do this, without risk to themselves and the people who they associate with."

"You talk about fighting the Krys as if they are helpless animals to be put down. Have you ever come to blows with one, General?"

He shook his head. "I am glad to say never."

"Precisely. Even without any weapons, they are highly dangerous opponents who should not be toyed with."

"Then don't toy. Go in there like you always do, and get the job done."

They were both quiet for a moment. Taylor could see there would be no getting out of it.

"And what if I left the Corps?" he asked.

The General's face sank in surprise and horror.

"Why on Earth would you think of doing that?"

"I am entitled to. I have done my service, and then some. I can put in my papers and be out of here before the month is through."

"But why? Not because of this fight? What is it you want? A rise?"

He shook his head.

"Then what?"

"To not have to put up with this bullshit. To not have

weasel little bastards like Weaver breathing down my throat, and being pulled around like some puppet to give crappy displays for an unappreciating public who want nothing more than to see blood. This is not what I signed up for, and not what we fought for!"

The General's concern turned to anger at his comments.

"So what, you'll walk out of the only career you've ever known, and do what? Piss about drinking too much and trying to relive the glory days. You're a fighter, a marine; it's all you know how to be. Now you don't have to like these orders, but by God you will follow them. You can be nothing out there in the World, a bum with nothing to offer, or you can be a Marine officer and a hero. You may have done great things in the war, but it is the machine behind you that made that possible and has made you the celebrity you are today."

Celebrity? Christ that's the last thing I want. All I ever wanted in my years in the Corps was to have some kind of life with Parker, and now that's the one thing being held from me.

"All right, I'll do it. But this is gonna end badly. The Krys aren't some wild animals to be cut up in an arena. Mark my words, this is the worst thing to have happened since we won the war, and you will regret it."

"It's out of my hands, and not for either of us to decide. I must follow my orders, just like you must follow yours."

* * *

Taylor walked back into his home and headed straight for the closet and grabbed his kitbag. He turned around to see Parker standing opposite him in the hallway.

"Thought you'd be at work by now?" he asked.

"I booked these few days off to share with you, remember?"

He had already forgotten.

"What can I say? I have my orders."

She knew it was useless to argue with that, but she wanted to nonetheless.

"You have to take this up the chain of command. You aren't a machine. You can't keep working day after day."

"We did in the war."

"Yeah, but the war's over. We worked without rest because the survival of our race was at stake. Why do you need to do it now, except to just appease a few idiots?"

He nodded in agreement.

"When I get back, I'll take this up the chain of command and see what I can do. They can't run me like this forever. They want me to fight over in France. I think it's a bad idea, and I think they'll realise it pretty quick."

"Why France?"

"Ah, some publicity stunt, I suppose; recreate a fight of the war or some shit."

"So they are making a gladiator of you?"

"I guess."

"A little bit beneath you, don't you think?"

"Marines, are we not the gladiators of our day?"

"No, because we don't play to a crowd."

"Mmm," he grunted back.

"What's that supposed to mean?"

"Look, I don't want to fight about it. These are my orders. I don't like them either, but they are what they are. I promise once this is over, I'll push for a few weeks' leave, and we'll go somewhere nice."

"I don't want to go somewhere nice. I just want you."

It brought a smile to his face.

"And you'll have me. Just give me a few days."

* * *

Thirty minutes later Taylor was aboard the bridge of the Deveron and soaring across the World for France. The ship had almost become his personal transport for publicity purposes. The crew loved it, for it meant light duties and a heap of attention from crowds wherever they went. Jafar travelled with him as ever.

The crew discussed Taylor's fight with such enthusiasm and expectation of what was to come next. They seemed to have enjoyed the concept as much as the public had. He hadn't thought those who had served in the war would be so keen for it. Then he looked around and realised that whereas they had all done their part in the war, not one of them had to ever come face to face with a Mech.

"Ready to whoop some ass?" asked Captain Ryan.

Taylor continued to stare out over the Pacific in a world of his own for a while until his brain finally processed what was going on around him. He turned to the Captain with a puzzled expression and asked.

"Ever fought a Kry in hand-to-hand?"

Ryan shook his head.

"If you had, you'd know the answer. It's no joking matter."

Ryan seemed confused.

"I thought you liked nailing those bastards?"

"Yeah, when I had to. When they were destroying our world and killing my friends. Because back then I knew every one I killed would save lives. But now they have lost, they are nothing more than our prisoners. Fighting one is nothing more than an execution, and a dangerous one at that. It brings me no joy."

Several of the other crew had overheard his comments and went silent. Many looked sheepish for having been so enthusiastic for the fight now they had heard is thoughts. Several felt sympathy for him, but he knew deep down they would still watch the fight with delight.

"So what are we doing here? Why are you fighting?"

"That's a good question, and not one I have an answer for."

Ryan could see it was time to drop the subject and quickly shifted focus.

"So I see you're still carting Tsengal around. Is it really necessary?"

"Mechs being lined up for gladiatorial combat and executions, and you have to ask? Tsengal is the lone survivor from Colonel Chandra's mission. If he ever wakes, I want to be sure it's someone I trust who hears what he has to say."

"Why? We're all on the same side here."

As he said it, Weaver walked onto the bridge. Taylor gestured over to the civilian and whispered to Ryan.

"You sure about that?"

"How long until we arrive, Captain?" Weaver asked.

"Ninety minutes."

"You've really stepped on it," added Taylor.

"Yes, Sir."

He could see the military courtesy he was given bothered Weaver.

"We're on a tight schedule, Sir."

"Yes, the crowds around the World are eagerly awaiting your fight, Colonel," Weaver added.

The rest of the flight went by slowly, and he had to put up with Weaver's endless bullshit that the crew seemed to lap up. Taylor had to admit Weaver may be an asshole, but he was a great salesman. As they finally came into land, Taylor instantly recognised their location. It shouldn't have been a surprise to him, but it was an odd feeling to be returning to Paris once more.

Lines of flags tracked a path up to their landing zone with thousands of people awaiting their arrival. Much of the city was in a state of rebuilding, and only a few newly finished skyscrapers made up the skyline. They were putting down in the gardens before the Eiffel Tower. It was a one kilometre square area of land that had been given priority in the restoration of the city. Despite many streets around the perimeter still lying in rubble, the grass was impeccable and the paths and benches like new. Construction cranes mostly covered the damaged tower itself as the rebuild was being undertaken.

"Hard to believe, hey, Colonel, that the city could ever return to its former glory?" asked Weaver.

You were never there during the war, so how would you know?

However, he was overcome by a sense of nostalgia seeing it once again. Their landing was smooth, and as the engines powered down, they could hear the roar of the crowd.

"It's time to meet the fans," Weaver said.

Taylor sighed as he put on his beret and headed for the exit ramp. His image in peacetime had always been carefully managed. He wore his Reitech armour because it was how people expected to see him. He was hardly ever out of it. Weaver always wanted him to be seen as a conquering hero, and not a politician. Rarely did he see his dress uniform anymore.

As the ramp lowered, the warm fresh air swept inside,

freshly mowed grass and moisture from the sprinklers. It was refreshing. He faked a smile for the crowd. It was not only his job, but also his responsibility to be the hero the people expected him to be. As he stepped out, he went onto autopilot. He shook hands and responded to greetings, but an hour later when he was free of it, he barely remembered a single moment.

Finally spirited away into an army staff car, he noticed the sun going down. They had lost many hours with the time zone change coming over the Atlantic. The afternoon had gone, and he wondered if they could even do anything with the rest of the day.

"Guess I'm not fighting tonight, Weaver?"

The man responded with a sleazy smile before responding. "Far from it. This evening's fight is prime time television. You'll be fighting at midnight local time. That's 1800 hours back on the east coast, just in time for workers to get home from the commute and have something to watch before dinner.

"Sounds like a great family night in," he replied, not attempting to hide the sarcasm.

"Not like you need the rest anyway. As far as your body clock goes, you've not even done anything all day."

"Two days ago that video went viral, so how can this be going ahead so soon? No consideration given, no discussion, planning."

"No planning or consideration? This isn't the twentieth

century, Colonel. Things change on an hourly basis. This is a now culture. They got a taste of the action two days ago. Forty-eight hours of waiting and anticipation."

"Jesus, are people really that bored? Did we fight to save a civilisation whose greatest desire is to watch the next piece of broadcast shit?"

"I can see you're finally starting to get it now. Maybe having me around isn't so bad for you, after all, Colonel."

He looked out of the window to see a welcome sign to 'Parc des Princes'.

"A stadium fight? What is this?"

"This is entertainment. The new Parc des Princes was under construction and almost complete before the first war broke out. With a few repairs and changes, it's ideal for our purposes. One hundred and twenty five thousand capacity, and with all eyes on you."

"Just what I wanted."

"To be the World's hero? Any marine would give anything to be in your shoes."

"Not one who fought in the wars," he snapped.

"Cheer up, Colonel. This is your big moment."

They rolled up to the entrance where a red carpet had been laid out for his arrival, and camera crews and reporters lined up behind barriers for any chance of an opportunity get at him.

"Play to the crowd, Colonel. It's what you've been ordered to do, and therefore, what you're paid to do."

He'd never been a fan of actors, and in joining the Marine Corps, it was the last thing he had ever envisaged he might have to do.

"All right, if this is what the people want, I'll give them their pound of flesh," he said spitefully. He opened the door, and his face instantly turned to a fake smile as he threw both his arms up triumphantly, sparking a series of camera flashes and a roar of applause.

Some people might be in their element, but this sucks.

One of the American reporters pushed to the front and yelled their question the loudest, bringing many others to silence. "Bookies are giving you ten to one odds, what do you say about that?"

Taylor was taken aback by the comment.

"I didn't come here to lose," he replied with a smile.

Laughter erupted as he turned to Weaver.

"Ten to one? What have you got me fighting?"

"You'll see."

Weaver stepped in front of the Colonel to speak.

"That's it. You all came here to see our hero fight monsters, not hear him talk. Give him his rest, for he has a great challenge ahead!"

They walked through the crowds as the reporters continued to hurl questions at Taylor, and others reached out to touch him as they passed. Beyond the crowd, he could see sparks from welders and construction crews still working away to finish the structure. Chemicals filled the air from flooring which had barely set. He knew this had been a rushed affair. He just hoped it wasn't at the expense of his safety. As much as Weaver's job was to make him a publicity whore, he seemed to want him dead just as much.

The stadium staff led them through the vast unfinished complex and finally through a lavish doorway that opened up into what could only be described as a luxury apartment.

"Welcome to our Presidential Suite," one of them stated.

It was lavishly decorated and ten times to the size of his own home. Screens around the walls were showing video commercials from around the World promoting the upcoming fight.

"Make yourself comfortable. I've got interviews to do, lots of them," said Weaver. "You'll be notified at 11:30 and called for at 11:45."

Taylor nodded and lay down on one of the sofas.

"You will be ready, won't you?"

"Sure," he replied confidently, as if bored by the whole affair.

Taylor awoke to find he was being rustled by one of the local staff members. He reached up and grabbed the man by the throat instinctively as he was torn out of a deep sleep. He could see the look of terror on the man's eyes as he was starved of oxygen. He quickly released his grip.

"Don't you know not to startle a marine like that?" he

asked.

"Sorry, Monsieur, but we could not rouse you."

He looked at his watch. 23:47.

"Okay, let's do this."

He was stiff from having slept in his armour, but the rest had done him a lot of good. He was led out and down to the ground floor. Weaver was waiting for him, next to a trolley with the rest of his gear.

"Christ, don't you know how important this is?"

"No, I don't," he replied dryly.

"Millions of people around the World are waiting for you, and you simply can't be bothered?"

"If you're so concerned, you could always armour up and go in there yourself. I know I'd enjoy watching that."

It immediately silenced Weaver, but he was fuming with anger. Taylor paced up to the gear on the trolley, a helmet, an Assegai, and a shield.

"That's it, Weaver?"

"They want a fight, not an execution."

Taylor couldn't help but think when all his gear was on it wouldn't matter who was wearing it.

Do the crowds really want 'Colonel Taylor', or do they just want to see human versus alien? I wonder if many would ever recognise me were I not in uniform as I'm portrayed on posters and videos around the World.

He clamped the Assegai in its sheath to the leg of his exoskeleton suit and lifted his helmet onto his head before lifting the hefty shield onto his arm.

"Ready?" Weaver asked.

"I'll do this fight, but that's it. After this, you find another idiot to be your puppet."

"You just get out there and do your job."

Taylor turned and strode out down the corridor that led to the main stadium grounds. He could hear the roar of the crowds as they yelled and clapped. It was almost deafening. He'd never been in front of so many people before.

"And here he is, the man himself. Welcome the slayer of Demiran, the saviour of the World, Colonel Taylor!"

The commentator was an instantly recognisable voice. An American who seemed to commentate on every big fight he'd seen over the years. He had no clue of the man's name, but his voice was unmistakeable. He rambled on another five minutes about Taylor's exploits and the dangers he was about to face, but it passed through Mitch's one ear and out the other. He was focused on psyching himself up ready for the action.

In the war he had always been ready to fight, as survival had been on their minds every second of every day, but his last fight just days before had shown him his head wasn't in it. He blocked out the crowds from his mind, focusing on the weapons in hand and the thought of what he was going to face.

Gonna kill the alien bastard, gonna kill you, gonna kill you, gonna win, he was telling himself.

His hands began to shake a little as the adrenaline flowed through his body. His mouth went dry, and his breathing slowed beyond what was ideal. He had to tell himself to get the air in.

Breathe, breathe, focus.

A trickle of sweat rolled down his face and hit his already dry lips. It tasted horrible and only made him thirstier. He felt a hand clench his and try to lift it, but to no avail. He looked to his side to see the commentator in a white suit and matching bow tie trying to raise his hand for the crowd, but it was only going where he wanted it to.

"Come on," the man whispered to him, "They love you. Play to it."

He gave in and did as asked. He snapped out of his mind-focusing daze to look at his surroundings as he was paraded around for all to admire. He was standing on a metal stage thirty metres wide. Thick armoured clear plastic walls surrounded him and must have been ten metres tall. They were braced by steel supports around the outside of the structure. Floodlights created almost perfect balanced light with only a little shadowing. The floor had smatterings of alien blood. He was clearly not the only exhibit that night, but he was the headliner they had all been waiting for.

As he continued to study his surroundings, the commentator left the arena, and the wall sealed shut behind him. There seemed to be no way in or out now except going upwards. Knowing his Reitech boosters would allow him that was a relief. A section of the floor in the arena slid open, and a single Mech arose from beneath the ground. It was still shackled and made no attempt to break free. He wondered if that was because it didn't want to fight, or if it had simply accepted it had to wait for its opportunity to try and kill him. Its armour had been polished so much that the floodlights glinted off of it.

Weaver began spouting his orders over the comms, but Taylor shut it off. That was the last thing he wanted to hear.

"Ladies and Gentlemen, let the battle begin!"

The shackles opened, and the Mech rushed immediately at him. Like in the previous display, it was armoured but without any weapons. With no finesse, it rushed at him as if in the hope of trampling him where he stood. Taylor quickly twisted his body to void to one side and drove the Assegai up into its torso armour, driving up to the hilt so that the tip would reach its throat.

The creature froze where it stood as he ripped the blade out. Blood poured down its armour and spread across the floor. It went limp and collapsed lifelessly to the ground. It landed hard. The metal on metal clang echoed around the stadium from all of the speakers that relayed every audible decibel for everyone to hear. The crowd was silent and stunned.

Taylor looked over to the side of the arena where Weaver and a few of Ryan's crew were sitting. Ryan was clapping and found it hilarious, but he was one of the few. Weaver frantically beckoned for him to come over to the perimeter. He finally obliged, as there seemed no response from the audience in what was becoming an uncomfortable silence.

As he reached the perimeter, he could see small holes perforated in the wall, just enough so that sound could travel through.

"What the hell was that?" yelled Weaver frantically.

"What you asked for," he snapped back.

"No, you're here to put on a show. That was shit."

"Well, I did say you're welcome to take over."

Weaver's face reddened, and he was boiling over with anger. Taylor knew it was a dangerous move when he was locked in an arena with god knows how many more potential combatants.

"All right, Colonel, let's see how good you really are."

Taylor ignored him and walked off into the centre of the arena where he awaited the next challenge. He ignored the crowd but watched Weaver whispering to the commentator who finally broke the silence.

"Ladies and Gentlemen, well, well, well. Did you ever imagine our hero here could vanquish a mighty armoured alien without breaking a sweat? He truly is an epic champion. But alas, this challenge is simply not enough for such a man. Who wants to see him put to the test?"

The crowd screamed with excitement, appearing to have forgotten the first fight already. It certainly hadn't provided what they wanted or expected.

Knew it couldn't be that easy, he thought.

Everything he had been told suggested it was a one off, one-on-one fight, but he'd always suspected Weaver would screw him over.

The floor hatch slid open once again, and three Mechs arose from the ground. He was only thankful they were still unarmed, for although he made it look easy, he knew they were not to be underestimated. The crowd was still silent, eagerly waiting what they had all come there to see, a fight.

"Right, if this is what you want," Mitch whispered to himself.

The shackles slid off the Mechs, and they approached slowly together in a crescent shape. They were being cautious and working together, precisely what he didn't need. He circled a little to try and get one in front of the other two, but they wheeled around and maintained their formation.

"Okay, if that's how you want to play it."

He leapt to his right onto one at the flank. It swung for him, but he pushed the Assegai into its huge iron claw, stopping it dead. One of the others closed on him quickly. He kicked up his leg into its chest and fired the boosters on his suit. It launched it back and thrust him and his first opponent into the air and rocketing towards the barrier wall. They hit it hard, but the Mech took the worst of the impact. As they dropped to the metal floor, the crowd erupted into cheers and applause; this is what they wanted to see. This is what they came for, a gladiatorial match.

Mitch pulled the Assegai from the creature's hand and thrust it into its chest. He quickly pulled it out and thrust again to make sure. Having vanquished one, he turned to meet the others, but it was already too late. The one that had been left standing was on him. He lifted his shield as a huge punch came for him. It impacted square on and launched him back against the wall. The wind was taken out of him from the impact, but he was still standing.

He thrust when the creature came at him, but it knocked his weapon arm down and swung again for his head. He ducked under, and the impact hit the transparent screen with such immense force, it opened cracks in the surface layer that spread almost a metre in every direction.

A hammer blow followed it, intending to flatten Taylor. He thrust his shield up and braced it with both hands and took it head on. As soon as the energy was dissipated, he smashed the lower edge of the shield into the creature's knee joints and then forwards, knocking it off its feet. The crowd cheered as he spun out from under it and quickly covered some ground to get away from the wall.

In that instance, Taylor knew he had won the crowd

over, but he wondered what that was really worth. His heart was now thumping and adrenaline was making him pin sharp. He was starting to enjoy himself. Gone was the anger at having to be an actor. The challenge and the danger was the most excitement he could remember having in a long time. He wasn't sure if he should be enjoying it, but he couldn't help it.

One down, easy work now!

The two rushed towards him simultaneously. He took a few paces to one side to get them in line and blocking one another. As the first tried to strike him, he pushed his shield up and slung his body low and thrust down into its leg. As blood poured from the wound, he ripped the Assegai out and thrust it up into its abdomen.

Seeing its companion was finished, the last one grabbed the body that was still impaled in Taylor's weapon and threw it aside as it bore down upon him. He ducked down and slammed his shield up and over so that the creature was launched over him and tumbled hard to the floor the other side. The crowd revelled in the spectacle of it, and began to yell for him to finish it.

He answered their calls and rushed forward with lightning speed. His shield smashed the creature's attack aside. He leapt up into the air, and his Assegai pierced its faceplate. The Mech collapsed dead beneath his weight. The crowd were in such ecstasy as if they'd just seen a national team win a global competition.

Mitch got to his feet and threw his arms up triumphantly. He had enjoyed the contest, but he still wondered what the event could mean for his future, and the future of society, as he knew it.

CHAPTER FOUR

"Good fight," stated Jafar.

"You think?" responded Taylor sarcastically.

He rolled off the huge bed in the suite of the stadium where he had stayed after the fight. The evidence of last night's drinking was long gone with not an empty bottle in sight, but his head was the only reminder he needed. His eyes took a while to focus, and he found Jafar standing just a couple of metres away watching him.

"It's still weird, you know, waking up to find you looming over me."

"Why?"

"Well... come on, we've been through this a hundred times...I give up. You got that car ready?"

"Yes."

"All right, then give me a few minutes, and we'll make a move."

"Where?"

"To see an old friend."

* * *

They soared through the French countryside. Parts were luscious and green, but other areas remained a wasteland compared to what they once were. They both knew Weaver wouldn't be happy about them vanishing from his sight, but that only pleased Mitch further. It was just the two of them and a driver from the Deveron.

"You know who lives out in these parts?" asked Taylor.

"Captain Jones?"

Taylor looked surprised.

"Well... yes, actually."

He didn't care to ask why but was a little curious.

"Yes, he retired last year to live out here with Sergeant Dubois. She saved our asses once, maybe twice. That was a life time ago."

"But he does not want a fighter's life, so what do you want from him?"

"Maybe a little reflection on life. These last few years are not what I imagined for myself, whether in or out of the Corps. He's away from it all."

The address Taylor had led them to a farm entrance in a secluded area where the wildlife seemed to be all they could hear when they got out of the car. The house must have been more than a couple of hundred years old and appeared completely untouched by the wars that had ravished the country so fiercely. There were no cars in sight, or anything that had been made in Taylor's lifetime. It was like stepping into a time warp and coming out a hundred years back.

"Not the kind of place I ever expected to find him," Taylor said.

"Freeze!" a voice yelled.

It came from where the car had parked.

Taylor's hand instinctively reached for his handgun, but the second shout brought him to a halt.

"Don't even think about it, you son of a bitch!"

He recognised the voice now and turned with a smile.

"You almost had me there," he replied.

He turned to see Jones behind their car with a gun to the driver's head.

"What are you doing here, Colonel?" he asked suspiciously.

Taylor was surprised by his tone. The hostility was not at all what he had been expecting when reunited with one of the friends he would hold dearest in the world.

"No way to greet a friend, Charlie."

"Whatever you want from me, I'm not interested!"

They heard another weapon cock and turned to see Dubois coming out from the side of the house with gun in hand.

"Not quite the warm welcome I was expecting," Mitch whispered to Jafar.

"I don't care what the offer is, I'm still not interested!" Jones shouted.

Taylor couldn't believe what he was saying. He began walking towards his friend.

"What the hell happened to you, Charlie?"

"Not another step!" he screamed.

"If you're here to recruit me, go away!"

Taylor was starting to understand.

"Not for a second. I just wanted to see an old friend."

"You sure about that?"

"Yeah, sure as hell," he replied calmly.

Jones lowered his weapon and walked out from behind the car.

"The slightest sign you're trying to get me to join you in some crazy thing, you are outta here."

"Got it."

"All right, then come with me."

He led them around the side of the house to a decked area with a table and chairs set up and a wide parasol giving shelter from the warm sunrays. Jones opened a small storage cupboard beside the house to reveal a refrigerator and threw a few beers out to them.

"Hell of a place you have here," said Taylor.

Jones sat down suspiciously and gestured for them to do the same. Dubois took a seat beside him.

"We saw your fight last night," she said.

Taylor had nothing to respond with.

"That's what being a marine has boiled down to? Blood sport?"

"Can't say I like it either, Charlie, but I have my orders."

"We both know you have done more than your fair share for the Corps and for the World. Why not leave? We did, and look at what we have. When we were huddled away at night, scared and expecting to meet our deaths at any moment, having to risk our lives every second of every day, this here is the life we dreamed of."

It was a compelling argument. General White had made him feel that without the Corps he would have nothing, but Jones made a lot of sense. One last issue bothered him, though.

"And when the next war comes, what then?"

"The next generation will fight it. None of us are immortal. We have done our part."

"So you would do that? If another attack came tomorrow, you would sit by and watch?"

Jones had to think about it for a moment.

"I would do whatever I had to do, but right now, we have earned this peace, and we are going to enjoy every second we get."

Taylor nodded in agreement.

"So you really didn't come here to recruit me into some scheme?"

Taylor shook his head, "Can't a guy just come for a chat?"

"I guess, just didn't see you as the type."

"Yeah, thanks."

"So you're going to keep fighting in these ridiculous displays?"

"I don't know. I don't want to. I shouldn't have to. But if I don't, I'll be outta the Corps before you know it."

"I don't think they could get rid of the famous Colonel Mitch Taylor so easily. But even if they could, so what?"

It gave him something to think about.

"When the World goes to shit and you really need me, you give me a call. Until then, I suggest you kick back and enjoy this life we earned for ourselves."

Taylor couldn't help but feel they were intruding on the life the two of them had made together. He finished his beer quickly and got up to leave.

"Great to see you again, Charlie."

He didn't seem disappointed they were leaving.

"Good luck in whatever you do, Mitch. Just know that you have done enough. It's time you started living for yourself."

Taylor got back to the car and slumped in the back with Jafar. He could not help but feel disappointed. 2nd Inter-Allied, the great Immortals, seemed to be nothing more than a fading memory.

"Is that the life you look forward to?" Jafar asked.

Taylor shrugged. "No idea, why, you got any thoughts?"

"I was not born a farmer," he quickly replied.

It was all Taylor needed to know.

They once more soared across the countryside on their return to Paris. As they rolled up outside the stadium, Weaver came rushing out in a flap.

"Where the hell have you been?" he insisted before Taylor had even got both feet out the door.

Mitch glared back at him.

"I may fight for you, but you don't own me."

"What? There are press conferences to do. Audiences are desperate to hear from their champion, and we have new fights to prepare for."

The comment seemed to have gone over his head, or he chose to ignore it.

"One week. One week, that is all we have before your next display. Young men and women are queuing at the recruitment offices trying to join up, and we have sponsors throwing money at us. This could be the greatest boost to the Corps in decades and is exactly what was needed."

"Great," he replied, uninterested.

Weaver chose to ignore that also.

"Come on, I have interviewers waiting to talk with you. Let's get you inside." He looked over to Jafar, "You can head back to the Deveron and await further orders."

"No," Taylor shouted.

"No? What do you mean, no?" asked Weaver.

"I mean exactly that. I've done everything you asked of me, but the big guy stays with me."

He could see Weaver didn't like it, but it was hard to say no before dozens of public and reporters who had spotted them and were already approaching.

"All right, all right, let's go."

One week before another fight? Boxers get how many months before theirs?

The next week was filled with seemingly endless TV interviewers asking him the same questions in different ways and expecting him to be as enthusiastic as they were. The endless cameras and idiotic questions that pandered to the mindless obsessions of the average viewer were getting to him.

It was the morning of his fight that had been milked for everything they could possibly get out of it, and yet he still did not know his opponent. It was a carefully guarded secret, intended to build more hype than the last one. Who his opponent would be was the last thing on his mind. He hadn't heard from Eli since he had left things so badly, and just as she came to mind, his comms flashed with an incoming message. He answered it to be greeted with her face. He jumped to his feet and tapped a button for the video to project her image before him.

"I was just thinking of calling you, Eli."

"Of course, you were," she replied sarcastically but smiling, "How's it going there?"

"About what you'd expect."

She went silent for a moment. Clearly, she had something big to say.

"Go on, spit it out," he said.

"These fights, you know you've got to put to end to it, don't you?"

"What do you mean?"

"People over here are livid about them. Seems half the World loves it and wants all the blood they can get, and the rest want to set the prisoners free."

"Set them free? And do what with them?"

"I don't know, but it's getting ugly. There are protests outside the base everyday about it."

"But Weaver said it's doing wonders for recruitment?"

"Sure, I guess, but it's stirring up big trouble."

"What would you have me do?"

"Call off the fight. Tell them you're not doing it."

"On what grounds?"

"I don't give a damn what grounds. Your word still holds a lot of weight in the World. You make it public you are against this, and it could make a difference."

"And is that what you want, for it to be ended? That because of the fights, or because it's me fighting them?"

"Both."

He looked away, thinking it over. He shared her opinion, but he hadn't realised how bad it had gotten.

"How is this the first I have heard about the controversy

over these fights?" he asked her.

"No idea, presumably someone wants to make sure you don't see that side of it. Mitch, this is all gonna come tumbling down, and you are right at the centre of it. Get out."

He opened his mouth to speak, but the transmission cut off abruptly. He looked down to his comms. The signal had been completely lost.

"Goddamn it."

He paced over to a computer console in the wall and went to the comms channel to find it too was down. The timing seemed too coincidental. He raced to the door and out into the corridor. Weaver was approaching, and Jafar still stood guard at the entrance to the suite.

"Ah, Colonel, we've just lost comms. The local towers are being flooded by fans, and it's overloaded the whole area."

It sounded suspicious, but he could rarely tell if Weaver was lying, for he did so frequently and believably, it became hard to tell.

"Just an hour until your pre-fight conference where we'll reveal your opponent for the first time," he said with a smile.

"Yeah, great."

"Fight this one, and you'll be done for a while. You can go home and take a bit of R&R while other fighters rise to the challenge."

I've heard that before.

"There's talk of a weekly live show, starting with representatives from around the World competing in the arena."

Weaver was trying to usher him back into his room, and he obliged until he worked out what was going on. He shut the door after him, despite the man wanting to follow him in. Taylor walked to the far end of the suite where a large balcony overlooked the arena. He stepped up to the edge and looked down to see security staff patrolling. Then he noticed a cleaner sitting beside a ride-on device. What held his attention was the fact the man was talking on his comms unit. He lifted his own and tried to make a call, but there was nothing.

"Bastard," he said to himself.

He knew something was up, and it was time to make a stand. Time seemed to fly by as he ran it all through his head, and the knock finally came at his door. He went to it to find Jafar had not allowed Weaver to just walk in.

"It's time, Colonel. Your crowds await you."

He stepped out and walked on with the man he despised so much. He just talked endlessly, and Jafar followed closely behind.

"Now remember, people want a bit of excitement. We're going to have your opponent there now so that you can..."

"What? Why?" Taylor insisted.

"We've got something special planned for this one. People need to feel there is a challenge and some risk and excitement."

"Risk, for me, yeah."

"Come on, Colonel, it may be your life out there, but can you imagine what would happen to any of us if any harm came to you? We have to keep you alive no matter what, so don't worry."

They weren't particularly reassuring words, but they did reinforce what he knew he had to do. He was led to a conference hall in the stadium that was full of reporters. It was not lost on him the fact it was a totally sealed environment. If there were protests in place like Eli had mentioned, he'd never have seen them. Weaver stopped them for just a second and pointed his finger at Jafar.

"You can stay out here."

He looked to Taylor who nodded in agreement and then took up position beside two Gendarmes, the local para-military policemen who seemed uncomfortable as he towered over them. The press conference had clearly been ongoing for some time, and as Taylor entered, the commentator who resided over the last fight introduced him.

"I'd like to give a warm welcome to our conquering hero, Colonel Mitch Taylor. Come and step up here, Colonel."

He stepped up to find he was once more bombarded

by cameras and in the limelight that he never appreciated. Uncomfortable silence overcame the hall as they all waited for him to speak, and yet nothing came. He looked at the teleprompter across the room that was flashing to get his attention. It was yet another speech written by Weaver that he had never even got a glimpse of, until now.

Taylor tried to open his mouth, but the words were not coming out. He knew what he should say, but it would almost certainly condemn his career. As time crept by, the commentator leapt back to the stage to stand beside him and get things rolling.

"Colonel, were all very honoured to have you here, but I want to introduce his opponent. We've got something special for you all here today. I don't know if I'd give any applause, but I'm certainly very excited myself. I want to introduce to you one of the greatest soldiers in the Krycenaean army, one of Demiran's handpicked veteran bodyguards. He faced off to Colonel Taylor and his companions once before. He bears the scars of that fight and still stands to take on the man himself in single combat!"

A screen at the back wall slid open and there he was, just as he had said. Taylor felt his body tense for action as he recognized the ornate and agile armour, as Jafar had worn when they first met. The Mechs were dangerous, but this was the first time since meeting Demiran in personal combat he had felt an overwhelming threat against him.

The only weapon he carried was his sidearm, which made him feel woefully underequipped. The commentator continued.

"Second only to the world-destroying Demiran himself, these aides to the enemy leaders have been called 'Destroyers' by those who have met them in combat.

Destroyers? That's just been made up for effect.

"What do you say, Colonel, about going up against one of these fearsome Destroyers in a fair fight. No rules, close quarter weapons only, and last man standing wins!"

He stepped from the podium to allow Taylor to retake his place. Mitch was still uncomfortable about turning his back on what they were now calling a Destroyer, but this was his opportunity. He was being broadcast to who knows how many millions.

"Welcome to all of you and thanks for tuning in."

Weaver smiled, it was just as the teleprompter read.

"You know who I am, and you know what part I played in the wars."

Weaver looked to the prompter because he didn't recognise the line at all. He was pointing at the screen and miming a shout at the Colonel, but he was completely ignored.

"I know why you tuned in here today. You hate the Krys and want to revel in their deaths. We all endured great hardships at their hands, and who wouldn't want a bit of payback? But did I fight this war, did you fight this war, so that we could earn peace or not? All I ever wanted throughout the wars was for it to be over, but it isn't over for me. I understand why this blood sport seems appealing, but I can tell you for certain, this is not the way."

Weaver was running along the lines of reporters and tying to get their cameramen to stop, but the crews were too enthralled in the story to care what he had to say.

"I saw what Karadag and Demiran did to those humans who survived their wars, and this is precisely the kind of thing they would be doing now had they won. Are we no better than that? These fights make a mockery of all those who fought, served, and died against the Krys, and I will have no further part in them. If it costs me my career, it's time to draw a line and say we are not animals. We are not barbarians. We are humans. This is Earth, and we will not stand for it!"

The room was silenced once more. The crews were fascinated by the eye-opening speech, but he had no idea how the viewers were taking it. Weaver rushed up on the stage and tried to barge Taylor off the podium, but it had little effect with his strong stature and Reitech equipment he wore.

"As a representative of the US Government, I want to confirm that any and all words of Colonel Taylor are not condoned by the United States. We have organised this fight because you, the people, wanted it. I am sorry to say that Colonel Taylor is clearly not feeling well and will return to service after..."

Taylor's hand connected with his shoulder and launched him across the stage. He slid across the floor and crashed into the empty chair that had been placed for him. The press turned their attention back to Taylor but were utterly speechless.

"No, I am not the word of the United States Government. I am the word of a United States Marine. Countless friends and colleagues of mine died for the peace we enjoy today. Let's not sully their name any further with this."

Weaver got to his feet, and his face was red with anger, but Taylor had not noticed.

"Fine, if you don't want to fight, I'll bring the fight to you," he muttered under his breath.

He called in on his comms 'knock out the feed'. The live transmissions from the room immediately stopped, though in their fascination with what they were seeing the press had not noticed. Weaver leapt up to the Destroyer and whispered to him, "That there is Mitch Taylor, the man who killed your master. How would you like a chance for payback?"

He could tell the creature understood him and simply nodded in agreement. Weaver stepped around the back of the creature to where his shackle bands were connected to a reinforced post. A keypad was all it would take for Weaver to release the Destroyer, and through his anger he didn't give it a second thought.

Six digits were all it took to release a lethal alien soldier amongst the crowd. He no longer cared what damage it would do, only that it would go for Taylor. "You'll die or make great TV," he said as the bands retracted, and the creature was free. In their focus on Taylor, the crowd had not noticed Weaver's treacherous actions.

The Destroyer rushed across the stage. The crowd gasped in shock and surprise, but it was too late. It kicked full force forwards at Taylor who only had enough time to turn and see it coming at him. He was thrown across the room and struck the wall the other side. His armour saved his body, but his head was bare and smashed against the wall. He crumpled down limply to the ground.

Screams echoed around the room when the crowd realised it was not part of the show and tried to get to the doors. The Destroyer leapt from the stage and rushed for Taylor. Gendarmes flanking the room drew their pistols but had to push through the crowd to try and get a clear shot. Bodies were flung aside as the Destroyer smashed his way through the press. It had no interest in them besides getting them out of the way, but several were killed from the sheer force as their necks were snapped.

As the alien reached Taylor, two of the police jumped in front of him, opening fire with their handguns. The rounds ricocheted of the creature's intricate armour and barely slowed it at all. The gunshots were enough to awake Taylor from his unconscious state. He was quickly reminded of how he'd got there and tried to shake off the drowsiness. Just as he got to his feet, the two Gendarmes with thrown aside like ragdolls. He drew his pistol and raised it to fire at the creature's exposed head, but it dipped its body slightly, and the two shots he fired went into the fleeing crowd.

In a flash it was on him and smashed him back against the wall. His pistol flew from his grasp, and he was lifted up against the wall. He tried to raise his knee to strike but couldn't get any leverage with his feet off the ground. The Destroyer's hands reached up and around his throat, and he knew he had just seconds before it would snap his neck.

He took hold of one of the fingers wrapped around his throat and with all his force snapped it back, breaking the joint. The alien winced a little and released its iron grip, allowing him to shift his weight and drive an elbow down onto its collar. He followed it with two punches to the alien's face. It was enough to free him. He fired his boosters and flew over the creature and came to a rough landing on the stage, causing him to go into a roll before getting back to his feet.

Weaver was still on the stage and now looked white with fear. It was clear he was already regretting his decision to free the Destroyer. He stood between Taylor and the alien.

"What are you waiting for? Kill it!" he screeched.

What as asshole, Taylor thought.

He stayed put, trying to use every second he could to get his composure back, and was in no rush to help the man who had brought it all upon them. The Destroyer strode forward. Without breaking stride, he took Weaver's head in one of its hands and crushed his skull. His body went limp and collapsed where he had stood. Taylor wouldn't miss him.

With nothing to hand, Taylor picked up a metal chair and smashed it down on the Destroyer as it came at him. The impact barley knocked it aside, and it grabbed one of the bars, ripped it from Taylor's grip, and threw it to the side. He'd never felt so helpless in his life. Without weapons, the creature seemed invulnerable.

Just as all hope was lost, he heard a loud shout in the alien language he did not understand. They turned. Jafar was standing equidistant to their side.

Thank God!

"You ready for this?" he asked his friend.

Jafar said nothing. He only rushed at the Destroyer. As it punched forward for him, he angled his body away and drove a knee in hard before pulling back and delivering a thunderous uppercut to it. It lifted its feet off the ground and fell on its back.

Taylor jumped in to stamp down on its head, but the alien nimbly rolled out of the way and back onto its feet. This was a long way from the clumsy Mechs he was used to fighting. It moved like Jafar and not so differently from Demiran. As Jafar approached, it spun out and struck its backhand into his face before lunging for Taylor. He jumped out of the way and rolled back across the room to where he could see his pistol resting.

The Destroyer tried to follow, but Jafar took one of its arms and pulled it back towards him. Taylor got to his gun and took it in hand. He turned back to see the sharpened elbow armour of the Destroyer strike Jafar and open up a huge cut across his cheek and onto his nose, but that didn't stop his friend coming right back at the beast.

As the Destroyer swung for him, Jafar took its arm and spun around so it locked the other also from behind. For just a few seconds, the alien was pinned. Taylor seized his opportunity and jumped in front of the two of them and put his pistol under their opponent's jaw. He did not hesitate to pull the trigger. Blood sprayed up and over Jafar. The body went limp, and he threw it aside.

Taylor breathed a sigh of relief as he wiped the sweat from his brow and found his own blood trickling down his face from the impact he had taken.

"Way too close," he muttered.

He looked down to the body of Weaver which lay face down. His skull had collapsed inwards in places, and there was no doubt he had died instantly.

"Bastard almost cost us our lives, and for what?"

He looked around the room to see another ten dead,

and six lying wounded from where they had been tossed aside with broken limbs from the impacts of the powerful creature. Camera equipment lay scattered across the floor. Two Gendarmes stood at the doorway frozen and speechless. They were the same two Jafar had loomed over when they first arrived. They had rightfully understood they could do nothing to help in the fight upon see the bodies of their two comrades.

Footsteps pounded down the corridor behind them, and a fire escape door burst open with another dozen Gendarmes rushing in through the side. They all stopped in shock like the first two. It took them a moment to fathom out what had happened. Finally, one of the new arrivals yelled.

"Do not move. You are under arrest!"

"No!" shouted one of the two who had been there throughout, "They, saved us."

The latest arrivals still couldn't figure out what had happened, and it was clearly a surprise to them to find an enemy soldier there at all. Taylor knew he had to speak. The man who had come to their aid was still too shocked to explain. He stepped up to the man who intended to arrest them. He looked at their weapons and saw they were the same outdated cased ammunition weapons they started the first war with.

"What do you expect to do with those pieces of junk?" he asked.

"We are here to police humans," he replied sternly.

"And if we hadn't been here to deal with this, what would you have done then?"

The Gendarmes officer leaned in close. Taylor could see an unmistakable burn mark running down his neck and inside his uniform, one that would only have been caused by a Mech weapon. He whispered so that only Taylor could hear.

"With all money being spent on redevelopment of the city, there is a limited budget for this. Not my choice of equipment, but given these or nothing, what would you have them carry?"

He felt sympathy for the Frenchman who was clearly only trying to do the best by his troops.

"So what happened here?"

Taylor pointed to Weaver.

"That idiot, my public relations clown, let that thing loose. It should never have been here in the first place."

"And you took it down with one pistol between the two of you?"

Taylor nodded. The man was surprised but didn't question it any further.

"You are currently stationed here?"

Taylor nodded once again.

"Then I would ask you stay here until we can pursue more inquiries as to how this happened."

Taylor agreed, but he was really starting to grow weary

of the place.

"I'll be in the Presidential Suite for twenty-four hours at the most. After that, I am out of here. Now this circus is over, it's time to get home."

"Yes, you must have many questions to answer."

Taylor had almost forgotten the subject of his discussions that had led to the violent turn of events. It was a heavy weight on his shoulders now that he had a moment to think upon it.

"You're with me," he said to Jafar, "I don't want any vigilante idiots turning on you."

In all honesty, he knew Jafar would provide more protection for him than the other way around, but he didn't say it.

"Good work back there, saved my ass. Last time I go anywhere without my Assegai, though."

Jafar agreed, and they strolled out from the conference hall. There was little sign of life except for the Gendarmes, for everyone else had fled for their lives. However, one civilian stood confidently awaiting them. He wore a suit and had his hands in his pockets and his feet spread wide in a relaxed posture. His hair was carefully slicked, and he seemed to want to present an easy-going image while still being all about business. Taylor had never seen him before, but he seemed to know the Colonel.

"Colonel Taylor."

"Who wants to know?"

The man smiled as if to be friendly, but it came off a little false. Taylor already knew he wanted something from him.

"Whatever it is, I'm not interested."

"No, you misjudge me, Colonel," he said, putting his hand up to stop Taylor in his tracks.

"I just want to talk."

"Right, thirty seconds."

The man launched into a speech he'd clearly had prepared for their meeting.

"I am Councillor Armand, UEN."

Taylor was both surprised and curious.

"Keep talking."

"I heard what you had to say in there. This gladiatorial combat being barbaric, and I can see here you have made a friend of one who was previously an enemy. I represent a substantial move with the UEN who is looking for a sensible and humanitarian solution to the alien Prisoner of War issue."

Taylor groaned. It sounded a little soft for him, but he let Armand continue.

"All we're looking for is a peaceful and sensible solution to the post invasion dilemmas the World now faces, but we need support from those who the World will listen to. Your voice holds weight, Colonel. Do not let it go wasted."

He handed him his business card. A small clear data card that Taylor had no doubt contained more information than he ever cared to investigate.

"If you want to see change, want to see some return to normality, contact me. I believe we have a lot in common."

The man turned and left, leaving Taylor with a hundred and one questions. It was a good strategy because it had worked. He wasn't at all sure what part Armand had to play in it all, but he knew it would not be the last he would see of him.

CHAPTER FIVE

"And breaking news, a battle has broken out in the conference hall at the Parc des Princes stadium in Paris, the location at which Gladiatorial games took place last week. There are mixed reports that alien sympathisers were involved in what could be a terrorist act, while others say alien Mechs were in a clash that left a number of dead and wounded. More to follow."

That was what Taylor had to wake to after an afternoon kip in his suite. The comms unit on the wall was flashing and had been for several minutes, but Jafar had made no attempt to answer it. Finally, Taylor got to his feet and accepted the call, finding General White's secretary at the other end.

"Please hold for the General," she stated.

He appeared a split second later and had obviously been waiting impatiently for a response.

"What the hell is going on there, Mitch?"

"Weaver went off the rails. Released one of Demiran's Destroyers... or whatever they're called in the press conference. It went crazy. Killed him, and did its best to kill me. Got a few civilians and cops on the way."

"Christ," he said, dipping his head into his hands.

"This was supposed to be a PR stunt, and it's a fucking disaster."

He went silent as his mind mulled over the situation and tried to find some answers.

"You sure that's the way it happened? There's talk of terrorism. It'd be a lot easier to explain than our man going psychotic and getting civilians killed."

"That's how it happened, Sir."

"And you, how did you survive?"

"Barely."

"This could put us in a world of hurt. We're gonna have to shift emphasis over to Weaver. He caused this shit, so he can take the blame for it, not like the stupid idiot is around to clean up the mess. Distance yourself from this, Colonel. There's trouble coming with this POW situation. At least we have comparatively few over here."

"So that's it? Dig our heads in the sand. Pretend none of this happened and ignore it all, Sir?"

"Bet your ass that's what you're gonna do. You're gonna stay there a few days until this situation calms down and then quietly slip out of there. Come back home, have that leave you deserve, and move on."

Sounds like a plan, he thought.

"We're gonna chalk this one up to a failed concept and get past it. Less we hear about it now, the better. Report to me when you get Stateside."

The transmission cut off, and Taylor could not help but feel he'd been ripped off. He'd risked his life and put everything he had into Weaver's concept, and he'd not got as much as a compliment on his work or a thanks for his efforts.

"Nice to know my life can be gambled on a clever idea, isn't it?" he asked Jafar.

The alien grunted and seemed to be indifferent.

"Yeah, that's right. You like fighting, and death means nothing to you. Great."

There was no response.

"Is there no way to get a rise out of you? Nothing I can do that will ever piss you off enough to get angry?"

"Why would you?"

"Curiosity, maybe."

The sarcasm was lost on him, and the room was left in silence.

"This is a fucking disaster, all that work and effort, and for what? We're stuck over here having risked our lives for nothing. Bring back the wars, I say. I'll take them any day over this misery."

He knew Jafar would agree, anyway. He always agreed

fighting was favourable over all else.

"I've had enough of this. There's not even a thing to drink in here. Let's find a bar."

"And the General's orders?"

"The last orders I got from the General almost got us killed. He's cutting all ties with this. As long as we get back home in the next few weeks, he'll be happy. All the years we fought over this country, and yet it seems we don't have a friend left in it."

Taylor stripped off his armour and was glad to be free of it. His BDUs still displayed the dried blood around the collar from his fight before, but he didn't care anymore. They strode out of the suite to find no one before their door. Not a guard to protect them, nor keep them in place.

"From celebrity to forgotten in five minutes. Can't say I'm complaining," he stated.

Ten minutes later they were walking into a nearby bar, in what felt like a repeat of the events that had led to the brawl and subsequent night in police cells so recently. Exactly as before, many of the patrons turned to stare at them, Jafar in particular. Taylor sighed at how boring this scenario was becoming.

"Yes, he is an alien. I am Colonel Mitch Taylor and this is Jafar, one of my most loyal colleagues. If you have a problem with any of this, then make it known now! Otherwise, should you say nothing and then cowardly make an attempt against…"

He drew his pistol and held it up for all to see.

"I'll shoot the first bastard who lays a hand on either one of us and not hesitate to shoot a few more. We did not fight over this country to put up with any bullshit. Now, can we sit down and enjoy a few beers?"

"Of course, Monsieur Taylor!" yelled the man behind the bar.

"Makes a change," he muttered to Jafar.

Grunts of approval echoed around the room, and several beckoned for them to come forward. It was the warmest welcome Taylor had ever gotten when Jafar was by his side.

"It's an honour to have you here, my friend," said the barman, "and this friend of yours we hear so much about. I don't know why you fight for us, but I thank you."

He passed two beers over the counter and didn't ask for any payment. Taylor was speechless.

"My brother said he met you once during the war. You would not remember him, but he certainly remembers you."

"Where did he serve?"

"All over, a trainee doctor he was then, volunteered as a field medic."

"And now?"

"Army doctor, he made it a career!"

Taylor had been waiting to hear the bad news that he had been killed in the fighting there, as so many stories he heard around the World. He was already starting to like the place.

"Paris is a lot easier to like when you aren't having to fight over it," he replied.

The Frenchman nodded in agreement. In the background a TV projection was running, and a nearby patron called over in French. He was obviously asking for the volume to be raised. Taylor looked and saw he was once again on air.

It was his speech from the conference hall moments before the battle with the Destroyer. The bar fell quiet as they watched it, realising it was the man sitting before them. Taylor's name had become widely known worldwide, but few would recognise his face.

The video came to an end with the screams in the room, and the signal cutting off and returning back to the news anchor speaking in French, of which Taylor understood nothing.

"What are they saying?" Taylor asked.

The barman looked uncomfortable, continued watching, and tried to translate as it went on.

"They are saying you are creating…divides, amongst different groups. Some are calling you a hero and humanitarian, and others, a coward and alien sympathiser…"

"Figures."

"Seems like you have created quite a stir."

"And you, what do you think?"

The man looked surprised to be asked his opinion at all.

"I...I don't know. I wanted peace for my country. Beyond that, I don't care. If people want to watch fighting on TV, then let them."

It wasn't a particularly helpful response.

"So, look here a second," Taylor said, pointing to Jafar.

"This is Jafar, an alien, a good friend of mine, and worth more than a platoon of fighters from most armies in the World. Do remember he is an alien? What we are saying here is, he is really no different from one of us. He fought for us, lives with us. Would you have him fight to the death in the arena and be butchered like an animal?"

The barman looked confused and sheepish.

"I don't know. It's not my place to say."

"But it is! Watch the TV. It's public opinion which is deciding what we should do next."

"Maybe, Monsieur, but are you sure anyone really cares about public opinion that much?"

It was food for thought. The report was still on going, and the barman continued to translate for him.

"They are saying it was an alien who got loose at the stadium and caused many deaths, and that local authorities subdued the creature."

"Local authorities?" Taylor laughed.

109

"They say there are growing calls to eradicate all remaining Krys on Earth, in an attempt to remove the threat to the public. Apparently, a number of leaders have signed a charter pushing for it at the UEN."

"Shit, this is really kicking off."

They heard a bottle smash at their side, and three angry looking locals approached.

"How'd we know this one wasn't in that stadium killing humans?" one asked.

"He was there all right, saving lives."

"I don't like Krys, and I don't like enablers like you. You're a disgrace to our race."

Taylor had heard enough. He drew his pistol and fired a shot through the man's leg. He cried out in pain. His leg gave way, and he dropped to the floor, screaming in pain. The other two men went to move forward but stopped, finding themselves staring down the barrel of his gun.

The rest of the room had silenced, and all that could be heard were the man's screams. Everybody was too shocked to go to his aid immediately and could only stand in amazement at what had happened.

"Monsieur, please, that's enough," pleaded the barman.

Taylor knew that anyone else from his unit would have held him back, but Jafar simply stood and waited for a response from the rest of the crowd. Mitch knew it was an extreme measure, but he had become sick of the constant harassment everywhere they went.

"You know everywhere we go we have to put up with the same assholes. Doesn't matter what country, what city. Does nobody care that this alien fought on our side, that he was vital to our efforts in defeating them? That you can sit here today and enjoy your drinks because he was at my side fighting?"

There was no response, though a few lowered their heads in shame.

"No one else here feels that way, but you can't just go shooting people," said the barman.

"The people wanted to see blood. They got blood…I never wanted this. All I wanted was to go home and get on with my life, but at every turn there's an asshole like this. Enough!" he screamed.

He knew he was losing it, but he could not help himself through the anger he felt towards so much of the World that had turned on him and his friend because they were no longer needed, because there was no longer a war to fight.

Sirens rang out in the background; the local police were bearing down on the establishment. Taylor necked the beer and walked out with Jafar at his back. Two police cars slid to a halt, but the officers relaxed when they recognised the two of them.

"We'll handle this," said one and allowed them to pass.

"Nice to still have a few friends," he replied.

At least that wouldn't make the news, he thought.

They returned to his suite. Taylor knew it was the only place they would remain trouble free as the General had ordered. Another day passed, and they tried to find anything to do to pass it. The stadium grounds were their prison for now, but they made the best of the space they had. Running, training, watching TV; it was all they had. On the morning of the second day, they were in the field grounds at one end away from the arena Taylor had fought it. They'd dug out a baseball and bat, and Taylor was throwing curve balls that Jafar was hitting so hard, they occasionally cracked the protective screens around the arena where he was aiming. It was all they could do for another few days until they could get out of there. Just when they thought they'd been left alone to pass the time, Taylor heard his name shouted.

"Colonel! Colonel!"

One of the Gendarmes he'd seen in the conference hall during the fateful event with the Destroyer was rushing towards him.

"Great, what now?" he muttered.

"Sir, I think you should see the news."

Taylor lifted his Mappad, switched on the projection display, and hit the shortcut to the World News Agency. The screen was filled with protest banners and scenes of mass crowds.

"Where is this?"

"At one of the prisoner camps in North Africa, but

there are scenes like this at another dozen locations."

"What do they want?"

"To exterminate the remaining alien prisoners on the planet."

"What?"

"Can't say I blame them, Sir. Those things are fucking dangerous, save your friend here."

He continued watching the news broadcast for a few minutes in amazement as the anchor continued to appraise the situation.

"While opinion is divided on the subject, it is up to the UEN now to come to some agreement on the subject of the alien prisoners. Pressure has mounted over coming years on action to take, but the UEN is yet to implement any initiative beyond maintaining the Prisoner of War camps. Many people around the World are beginning to question if money and resources should be allocated to an enemy which once tried to destroy humanity."

"This is gonna get ugly," said Taylor.

The day continued much as the previous had. Nobody seemed interested in reaching Taylor since the debacle at the stadium, that or they simply didn't know how. Taylor took off his uniform and lay down on the ridiculously oversized and lavish bed in his suite. He dreaded waking up the next morning. He knew trouble was coming, and there was no doubt he would be drawn into it.

As the sun rose, he awoke naturally. For a moment,

everything seemed peaceful. The World hadn't ended, and he'd caught up on some much needed rest and recovered from his minor injuries, but the pleasant morning wouldn't last. A chime rang to signify somebody at the door, and Jafar was quick to answer it. It was almost as if the alien had defaulted to being his butler and manservant, a situation he was not comfortable with.

The door slid open, and the same Gendarme who had delivered yesterday's news rushed in.

"Sir, I really must warn you. Crowds are gathering outside the stadium and protesting your presence."

"What are their intentions?"

He shrugged his shoulders.

"Thank you for your concern, and please keep me notified of any further developments."

The man nodded in agreement. Taylor wondered why he was delivering messages in person rather than through comms. He wondered if he was going outside of his job parameters, as he rushed out as quickly as he had come in.

"I don't like the sound of this at all."

He turned back to the news channel. A Spanish politician was being interviewed, and the topic was clearly the Colonel himself, for a picture was projected behind the news panel.

"What do you think of Colonel Taylor's latest condemnation of the treatment of the alien prisoners after having so recently brutally killed them for entertainment?"

"I think the Colonel is most mistaken in his apathy for these monsters. Maybe he is disillusioned with the bloodshed, or maybe mentally scarred from all that he has seen. No one can deny his great efforts during the war, but Taylor is very much that, a war machine, one which should stay out of politics."

"Strong words, and now onto Miss Patricia Nowak, a key representative in the Earth for Humans movement. What's your feeling on Colonel Taylor's surprise comments in Paris that have sparked so much controversy?"

"The Colonel's comments were way out of line. He of all people should understand the threat these invaders pose, and while he may have been a hero a few years ago, people change. His latest actions are those of a coward."

Taylor cut the transmission off. He couldn't listen to it any longer.

"How quickly they turn on you," he whispered.

He felt helpless now that they were shut away in the stadium. Then he remembered Armand and shuffled through his pocket to find the Councillor's card. He pulled out his Mappad and slipped it into the reader. His credentials came up and were immediately authenticated. His hand hovered over the contact button. A man he'd never met, and he was going to reach out to him for, well he didn't know what.

"What the hell," he said and put the call through.

Taylor was surprised to see Armand's face. It was a

direct line to the man personally.

"Colonel Taylor, what can I do for you?"

"I'm not entirely sure, but you must be aware of what's happening in the World. Something has to be done, and no one Stateside is interested."

"Stay put, Colonel. I'll come to you."

Taylor was surprised at the response and speechless for a moment.

"That...would be great."

"I'll see you shortly, Colonel."

The call ended, and Taylor put the news back on. He hated having to watch it but knew he had to stay abreast of everything that was happening. More scenes of protests filled the screen, and a reporter was being shoved around as she tried to talk into the camera.

"I'm here at the entrance to the Gafsa Prisoner of War Camp in Tunisia. Home to as many as ten thousand enemy soldiers, it is one of the larger prisons, and as a result, a massive draw to people calling for an end to their lives. Around five thousand protestors have gathered here so far, with more arriving every hour. People are calling for something to be done, but the authorities are nowhere to be seen, in a standoff which is looking increasingly dangerous for all involved."

Screams rang out, and Taylor heard the sound of two gunshots in the background. The camera turned to show a protestor fall from one of the perimeter fences. The video shook around as the crew tried to get closer and managed to get a partially obscured view of the man getting to his feet and looking in pain.

"It looks as if non-lethal ammunition has been authorised to be used against anybody who makes an attempt on the perimeter of this massive complex. Attempts are also being made to sway incoming pilots bringing in supplies to turn away, of which we have seen a few do so. Everyone here is looking for the authorities to do something. I am now hearing reports that pro-life alien sympathisers have also started demonstrations nearby."

"Look at them," said Taylor. "At each other's throats, and over what?"

"They are right, though. You can't keep that many enemy soldiers locked up forever."

"What would you suggest? We can't free them. They are the enemy. We can't kill them. That would be barbaric. And we can't send them home, as even if it was logistically possible, we can't return troops who would likely be sent right back against us."

"Death is the kindest option," Jafar replied quickly.

He was starting to see it wasn't as simple a problem to sort out as he first thought.

Death does indeed seem like the answer, but it's also the kind of genocide humanity has fought so hard against.

"Can we not sway them to our side, or at least live in peace, like you and I?" he asked.

Jafar looked highly doubtful.

"Would you risk it? A potential army let loose in the World in order to keep your conscious clean?"

"So this is it? The answer is to become like them and commit genocide so that we can live the lives we want to? I don't accept that."

A minute later, Armand was at the door. Taylor was surprised he could get there so quickly. He could see no reason why he'd been at the stadium unless he had been waiting for his call.

"How can I help you, Colonel?"

"You must have seen the news."

"Yes, and very disturbing it is, too."

"It's time we did something about it."

That tweaked the Councillor's interest, and it almost seemed as if he'd been waiting for days for Taylor to come out with such words of his own accord.

"As part of my duties in the UEN, I have been asked to head to Tunisia to some of the worst of these protests, and see if I can do anything to quell them peacefully. Having a famous face such as yours by my side could make all the difference. Your comments on TV have gained substantial support. Maybe not with everyone, but enough."

"And you think a marine could calm the environment down? It's not what we're intended for."

"I think you have forgotten your true purpose, Colonel. A marine fights for peace, not the continuation of war."

"Mmm," he muttered in response.

"Things are looking bad in North Africa. Will you give it a shot, and come with me or not?"

Anything to get out of here.

"Yes."

"Great, then there's no time to lose. Let's move."

He really has been waiting for my call.

Armand led them to the stadium grounds where a ship awaited them. It was a luxurious yacht and far from the simple military vessel the Deveron was. He seemed to be whisked away into yet another world he was unfamiliar with.

It was a short journey to Gafsa, and as they approached, Taylor could see a swarm of people at the perimeter walls. They flew right over the masses of civilians and came down to a landing pad just inside the walls. As the engines powered down, they could already hear the screams of the crowd even through the reinforced glass.

"This ain't gonna be easy," said Taylor.

"If it was an easy job, I'd not have got you on board," replied Armand.

"That's reassuring."

They headed down the ramp out into the warm open air where the crowd's roars drowned out almost everything. A small party that was armed greeted them on the landing strip, including the prison warden, an army officer of the rank of Lieutenant Colonel. He instantly recognised

Taylor and was uneasy in how to take his presence.

"Lieutenant-Colonel Spiteri, I hope you boys have some answers here because this is becoming a real shit storm!" he yelled.

They could barely hear him over the sound of the heckling crowds.

"Follow me!"

They did as he asked, and Taylor leaned in to Jafar.

"Why do we always end up in the shit?"

"Because you volunteer us," he replied.

Taylor wasn't sure if he was being straight or exhibiting sharp wit, but it made him laugh, either way. They passed beyond several guards into an operations room where the rest of the Colonel's staff were largely standing around with nothing to do, except talk among themselves. No one even called them to attention as the base commander entered, and it was already clear to Taylor that it was run as a very loose ship.

Spiteri beckoned for them all to join him and the newcomers at the operations table, which was blank. It was an indicator of how little they had done in any efforts to quell the problem.

"Gentlemen, this is Councillor Armand who is here to oversee negotiations with the protestors. As a representative of the UEN, he has complete access to the site and is accountable only to me. Colonel Taylor of the US Marine Corps is here as an advisor to Armand. I expect you to extend all courtesies to the Councillor and his associates. Right, now down to business."

A live satellite projection displayed on the table, showing both the vast breath of the prison, as well as the shocking large numbers of protestors which were gathering.

"The number of protestors is growing at an incredible rate. When it first began, we expected them to become tired in a day of the heat without supplies, and pack up and leave."

"Why hasn't that happened?" Taylor interrupted.

"Because of the aid they have been getting. Shuttles deliver supplies on an hourly basis, bringing them food and water, instant shelters, and mobile toilet and shower blocks. Somebody with big money is keeping this going."

"Or many people with a lot of money," Taylor added.

"It's sad but true," said Armand, "There are sizeable numbers opposed to what is going on here who would be willing to pour money into other's pockets to oppose it for them."

"And people used to protest against people being kept in these kind of prisons," muttered Taylor.

"That's right, Colonel. They protested about people being locked up, but this is an entirely different story. If you hadn't noticed, aliens exist and want our planet," said Spiteri.

Taylor wondered if the man knew who he was and his history in the wars, but before he could ask, attention was turned to the elephant in the room.

"And please can someone tell me what the hell he is doing in uniform, and with a US Marine?"

One of Spiteri's men leaned in and whispered in his ear.

"Okay, so you're that Taylor, a war hero. Well, let me tell you, I saw plenty of combat in the war myself, and I would never in a million years let one stand beside me and call a comrade."

"Be thankful I am not you then, or we might not have won this war."

Tension was getting to boiling point in the room, and no progress was being made, but Taylor didn't travel there to make idle argument.

"The local government must be doing something to alleviate the troubles here?" he asked.

Spiteri shook his head. "I wish. The war destroyed the populace in this area, one of the reasons it made such a good prison. A few thousand have moved back into a nearby town, but they are little more than a frontier site, like something out of your history. A sheriff and his deputies trying to manage the locals; they can't do a thing to help here."

"And the UEN?"

They all turned to Armand.

"The UEN is willing to consider deployment, only if wide-scale violence is a likely possibility. Besides that, I am all that you're gonna get."

"And what are you worth?" asked Spiteri. "Can you talk this horde down and make them go back home and forget all of this?"

"I'll give it a shot."

"A group that says they are in charge out there has been calling for a representative to meet with them for the last few hours."

"Good, that's a start."

"I'm not going out there, and I won't risk my men doing so."

What a fucking hero, Taylor thought.

"Fine, I'll go out there. Two of my bodyguards, and I'll take Colonel Taylor with me."

"And what about his...friend there?"

Armand looked over to the towering alien and then over to Taylor.

"We can't take him. He'll only pour gas on the flames. He can stay here. I'm sure Colonel Spiteri will ensure his safety."

Taylor almost laughed but held himself back.

Not his safety you have to worry about.

He nodded for Jafar to stay put, and it was a message clearly understood as he paced out into the blistering sun with Armand and his guards.

"You really have a plan here?" he asked.

"It's all just a game, Colonel. Hear what they have to say, and find a way to oppose it."

"Not really a negotiation, is it?"

"That's exactly what it is."

The inner gates opened and shut quickly behind them. They were sealed off from the base now, with only four of them soon to be heading out into an angry mob.

"We're coming out to negotiate!" Armand shouted.

"Not with weapons you're not!" one replied.

They looked out at the overwhelming odds. He looked back to Taylor for an answer and saw the Colonel shaking his head.

No goddamn way.

They stood there silently until the protestors at the gate accepted it was the only way they would see some progression. The gates slid aside, and they stepped out into the hostile crowd who seemed as if they wanted to kill the four of them as much as the aliens inside.

They were led through the crowd, hundreds of men and women who glared at them as if they were criminals. Taylor hated the way they peered down at him.

The only reason you're alive today is because I fought for you.

But he fought the desire to say it aloud with all his fibre.

They eventually reached a structure. Internally, it was not so different to the operations room he'd recently left. A dozen men and women stood around a table, planning and discussing their actions.

"More like a military operation than a protest," he said

to Armand.

"That's right, Colonel!" one of them replied, overhearing him.

"And you are?" he asked

"My name is of no consequence. You can call me X."

You're wearing the pants here, then.

"My name is…" began Armand.

"We're not interested in your name. Our demands are this; the instant euthanization of all prisoners of this facility and all others like it. That is the only thing we ask. We will not accept anything less and require nothing more. Are you ready to provide what society is calling for?"

"I am willing to negotiate the matter, but there has to be some give and take. Let's start from a middle ground and work this out," said Armand.

"You heard what I said. What part did you not hear?"

Armand seemed speechless as she turned her attention to Taylor.

"Colonel, we know who you are, a great hero of the wars. You must have killed so many of the invaders, do you not want to see an end to this?"

"An end? Yes, I thought I saw this when we won peace on this planet. We, and those who fought for it," he replied.

One of the protestors stepped forward, yelling at him. "I was there the day you killed Demiran and saw it with my own eyes. I served, I fought, I killed, and for what? It isn't over. We want life back to the way it was!"

"Then I am sorry to say that this negotiation is over. We are wasting time if you are not willing to discuss the matter in a civilised fashion," Armand replied sternly.

Taylor was surprised by his attitude. He appeared to have come there to resolve the problem, and yet seemed to have no interest in doing so.

"Then leave, and return to the living joke you call a detention centre," X quickly responded.

Armand turned and left without another comment.

Is he gonna fight for this?

The answer appeared to be no as he carried on. The Colonel was left with no choice but to leave with him. All they passed as they headed for the gates were constantly heckling them. Finally, a punch was thrown at one of Armand's guards, and he almost fell to the sand before lifting his weapon to his attacker.

Rocks began to pelt the guards from nearby protestors, and one hit the guard who have been shoved and broke his nose. It sent blood spewing over his uniform. He turned back to the crowd and saw more rocks hurling towards him. He opened fire.

"No!" Taylor called out desperately.

It was too late. The rounds were non-lethal but struck with immense force, and the people took it as red to attack. Several drew weapons, and one launched forward with a machete and struck down on the arm of the shooter. It cut deep and halfway through his forearm, but even that was not enough to bring it all to an end. The other guard had joined the fighting, and those within the perimeter had been monitoring the trouble and began to respond.

The non-lethal ammunition seemed to do little to hold back the crowd, many of who seemed to carry on as if nothing had struck them. Taylor could just make out the sound of notice being given over the tannoy system, warning of lethal force being authorised, and that did nothing to calm them.

Two of the angry mob came at him, and he had to fight every instinct that told him to draw his pistol and defend himself. Human blood was the last thing he wanted on his hands. He knew he must rely on his body for defence and the power the Reitech suit gave him. He struck the first with a punch that sent the man tumbling back into his friends.

A woman then came at him like a screaming banshee and wielding a truncheon-like weapon. He took hold of her and launched her into the mob the other side. He looked down to see Armand trying to stop the bleeding of the wounded bodyguard while the other fired wildly to keep them back. Clearly, his ammunition wasn't going to last long. Before Taylor could come up with a solution, gunfire rang out from the prison and ripped into the mass of people.

Some of them froze in panic while others charged at the fences, but it was a pointless act. Taylor could do nothing but watch in horror as dozens of the protestors were struck down by live ammunition. Then the path to the gates became clear, and he snapped back into action. It was his opportunity. He reached down and hauled the wounded man up as if he weighed nothing at all.

"Move!" he ordered Armand.

As they rushed for the gates, several of the armed protestors tried to get at them but were hit by aimed shots of the guards at the walls and watchtowers who covered their retreat. By the time they reached the perimeter gate, there was nobody on their trail, and they could see Spiteri waiting and watching behind the inner perimeter.

"Stop firing!" Taylor called to him.

He seemingly ignored the comment until they had got through the gates.

"Attend to that man!"

Taylor passed him over to medics and looked back. A few shots were still being made as the crowd tried to retreat but could not make it through the dense wall of their own people.

"Cease fire!" he finally yelled. He'd waited beyond a reasonable time, as a message to Taylor that he ran the place. "Send medics out and aid the wounded!"

Mitch looked out across the plain and could see a hundred bodies of the dead and wounded on the ground. This was a disaster, and he knew they would pay dearly for it. He wasn't sure how he'd got out from the mob, but he knew there would have been a better way.

"You just screwed us all," he said to Spiteri.

CHAPTER SIX

Six hours later.

"Sir, we have three incoming ships."

"What's so special about them?" snapped Spiteri.

"Sir, they aren't transports or Red Cross. They're UEN warships."

"What!"

The ships approached without a declaration of their intentions or request to land, but Spiteri knew he could do nothing but let them land and find out their purpose first hand. Taylor knew it was the reckoning for the Colonel. He prayed he would not be lumped into the whole affair.

The two of them paced out into the landing zone with a dozen guards and Armand close by Taylor's side. He still looked horrified by what he had seen and had barely spoken more than a few words since that time.

"What do you think they're doing here?" he whispered.

"You don't know?" replied Taylor.

"I came here as a negotiator, nothing more."

Taylor got the impression he knew far more than he was letting on, but he'd let it slide, considering recent events.

"UEN can't let this stand. If they leave Spiteri in charge, they'll have a tonne of bricks down on their heads. They'll want to distance themselves from him and his actions ASAP."

Armand didn't seem surprised.

"You do realise this is a disaster? Besides the obvious loss of life, it has given the protest movement all the fuel they need for this fire?"

"We can only do what we can do, Colonel. We are but human, after all."

Taylor was starting to get the impression he'd expected this to happen, and it had been part of his plan. If it was, it was far from his understanding yet. He looked over to see Spiteri was worried.

So you should be, you asshole.

From out of the ships poured UEN soldiers from Germany and a familiar face at their head, General Schulz. Military police flanked him also; something that still sent shivers down his spine. Taylor had learnt to tolerate and respect the General, but he'd never forgive him for his incarceration.

"Welcome to Tunisia, General…" started Spiteri, as the imposing force approached.

The General ignored his gesture completely.

"Lieutenant-Colonel Spiteri, under the authority of the UEN, I am relieving you of your command and placing you under arrest!"

Spiteri looked around to his colleagues, looking for some support, but none would stand against the General and his troops.

"Arrest? For what?" he pleaded. "For doing my job, for saving a Councillor's life?

Schulz ignored his comments and sent the MPs forward.

"All prison staff involved in the shooting earlier today are to hand in their weapons at the armoury and return to your billets, where you will remain under house arrest until notified over wise. UEN soldiers will take over perimeter guard duties for the entire facility!"

He looked over to Taylor and saw he had no weapon in hand.

"Colonel Taylor, I am told you did not draw your weapon during the incident. Is that correct?"

Before he could answer, Armand jumped to his aid.

"I can confirm that, General. He protected my men and me and did not use a weapon throughout. Two of my own were involved but used only non-lethal ammunition in self defence."

"Very well, Councillor. As key witnesses of the events here, you are both to escort the prisoner and me to Brussels where a full and immediate investigation is to begin. The

World wants answers."

"And the protests? We came here to negotiate to bring them to an end."

"Negotiations are over. My own soldiers will ensure no one else comes to any harm, both inside and outside the facility, while this is resolved."

The MPs removed Spiteri's sidearm and took up positions around him. His shoulders seemed to sink as it sunk in that he was in big trouble, yet he didn't seem to show any sympathy towards the dead and wounded or regret for his actions, only disappointment at his arrest.

Ten minutes later, Taylor was aboard yet another ship being whisked away to yet another country he had no interest in visiting, on a mission not at all suited to his talents. He had listened to Armand relay the entire events of the shooting within minutes of getting aboard.

Schulz seemed more interested in Taylor and turned his attentions to him.

"You've heard what Armand has reported to me, all of which has been recorded, will you corroborate his story fully?"

"It's what happened."

"So you agree with every detail?'

"It was a pretty simple affair, and yeah, I do."

"Then Spiteri is going down," replied Armand.

"It's not a victory," added Taylor. "Only another hurdle on the way to resolving this great big mess."

"Agreed, so let's get it done quickly. On arrival, you will be escorted to the Hotel Be Manos, along with Colonel Spiteri who will be kept closely guarded until the trial begins in the morning."

"Tomorrow morning? And a trial beginning without an investigation?" Taylor asked him, surprised.

"Prosecution teams and UEN investigators have already been working on it and will do so throughout the night. You've seen the escalation of protests in the World. People need to know we are acting in their interests."

"I've been on the wrong end of these events before. I can't imagine being condemned for life with so little time or thought."

"Then never open fire on and kill civilians."

Taylor could feel it was all going too fast. Anger was brewing on all sides, and rushing it was only going to cause brash decisions, but he felt powerless to stop it.

* * *

It was another short journey to Brussels, but the day had felt like one of the longest since the war. As Taylor wearily stepped inside the lavish room that had been selected for him, all he wanted to do was sleep. But first, he mustered up the energy to put a call through to Eli.

"What the hell is going on there? Are you okay? You said you were in Paris, but I just saw you on the news at that prison where the shootings happened."

"I'm fine."

"Fine? Turn on the news, Mitch, and look at what that shooting means to people. They're going psychotic over it."

"Not as a result of anything I have done. I was asked to go and help there, and that's what I'm still doing."

"Well, you better figure out pretty quick which side you're on."

"Side?"

"Have you not seen the news today?"

Been a little busy, he thought.

"The World is dividing into those who want the aliens executed and those who don't. They're at each other's throats. Riots have broken out in Washington and New York between the rival groups and in other cities around the World."

"I'm a marine, not a politician."

"Hardly," she replied. "You're out there on your own, making your own decisions. Out there you aren't a marine, you're a celebrity; one which both sides will be eager to recruit."

He shook his head, "How did it all go to shit so quickly?"

"The day aliens invaded," she replied.

"That's a big help," he said with a smile.

"Nothing good can come of this, Mitch. Get yourself out of it and home ASAP. We don't have anywhere near the number of Krys held over here. It's not such a problem. Get your ass out of it."

"Do my best."

"I love you," she replied.

He could hear the worry in voice, and he was starting to realise how serious the events were in determining their future. She cut off the transmission before he had time to reply. Within five minutes, his armour was off, and he was in a deep sleep, the best he'd had in a long time. The recent events weighed heavily on many minds, but he was simply content to never have to do the circus displays his job had become ever again.

* * *

A loud knock at the door awoke him from his sleep. He staggered over to open it and found Jafar standing there.

Does the alien ever sleep?

"Any news?"

"A conference has been called at the UEN."

"Great, another opportunity for politicians to bore each other to death."

"I don't think so."

Taylor was surprised and invited Jafar in, as he paced over and turned the news on. Every news channel seemed to be a live feed of the conference that was already heating up. The Italian President was almost screaming across the room at his peers at such a volume and strong accent, Taylor could barely make out his words. Fortunately, he finished up, and the French President was invited to talk, President Jacques.

"France cannot risk enemy combatants on her lands ever again, and must take any move necessary to remove that threat. As the representative of my people, I feel it my duty to call for the immediate execution of all enemy combatants held within EU lands, and a strong recommendation that the rest of the World see merit in doing so with all haste."

Grunts of approval and anger echoed around the room.

Taylor watched the conference for two hours. It seemed little more than a screaming debate between two groups who would never be swayed from their standpoints.

Finally, the Spanish Prime Minister arose and looked around the room, carefully studying the faces of all the representatives there. He clearly had something major to say, and all were silenced as they waited to hear it.

"The people of Spain will no longer tolerate the existence of murdering invaders on Earth. At 0900 hours tomorrow, Spanish time, two divisions of our armies will cross over into North Africa on orders to exterminate the enemy held there."

Heckles came from the crowd, but he only lifted his hand and waited to speak.

"The UEN has proven impotent to act on this matter

for four years, and we can no longer stand by and let this threat remain so close to our homes. Our forces will carry out these orders, and have strict orders to not be stopped by any force on Earth. Should any human stand in our way, we will have no choice but to do what we have to. We will protect our country and this World at any cost!"

"Oh, shit," Taylor said quietly.

"Your people are turning on each other?" asked Jafar.

The German Prime Minster, Ms Muller, leapt to her feet to address the issue.

"Our forces currently serve at those bases and have a duty to protect those within the prisons, as much as those outside them."

"Then have them redeployed, for nothing will stop out forces from doing their duty!" shouted the Spaniard.

Taylor could see they had reached deadlock as he continued.

"Any further discussion on this matter is wasting breath. No human is safe while an alien remains alive on this planet! Tomorrow, the men and women of the Spanish Army will do their duty to protect human lands across the World, and God spare any human who may stand in their way!"

He got up and stormed out of the room. Several other leaders followed suit, including President Jacques.

"Oh, we have some trouble on our hands now."

"Will they really kill each other over this?"

"We've a long history of doing so, why should now be any different? Even so, this all seems to be happening a lot quicker than I'd expect. A few months ago, the protests were an annoyance to local governments, now we're heading for war. It's as if we're being moved around like pieces on a board. Somebody wants this war, and there seems little we can do to stop it."

"What are you going to do?"

"Me? What the hell can I do? I'm not a President, Prime Minister. I supposedly have a Battalion, but have not seen them in a year. It's just you and me, and everywhere we go a fight starts."

He looked at his watch. Spiteri's trial was going to begin shortly, but there seemed little point, as he was going to face the full sentence for his crimes. He pulled on his uniform that had been cleaned by the hotel staff overnight and headed out the door to be met by armed escorts. It made him uncomfortable. He'd been escorted like this before, and it was right to a prison cell.

"Lead the way," he ordered.

The court was right opposite the hotel with a pedestrianized area between them. On entering, he was met by a guard who expected him to give up his firearm. He knew he had no choice. Jafar tried to follow him through the foyer but was quickly stopped.

"Authorised personnel only," said a guard.

Taylor nodded in response. He could fully understand

their position, considering the topic at hand. He was led into the courthouse to join the audience. Just five minutes later, Spiteri stood before them all. Taylor had only ever seen a few court cases in his life, and they never moved this quickly and with such single focus.

Spiteri looked utterly unashamed of his actions and stood tall in his dress uniform. Taylor still wasn't sure from which nation he came, but his query was soon answered as the judge introduced him as Maltese. Mitch had been one of the key witnesses at the scene, and one of the few who had no agenda towards the Colonel. He'd expected to be called up before the court quickly, but instead was surprised to see a recording of Armand recounting the tale and him agreeing with it.

"Is that enough to condemn the man?" he muttered to himself.

In three hours, they'd heard all there was to hear, including first-hand accounts from protestors who had been wounded at the scene. On the one hand, Taylor knew the man was guilty, but he couldn't help but feel sorry for him as he wondered how it could have been handled differently. He was also beginning to wonder why he was even required to be there, seeing as they had all the evidence they needed.

"The court is adjourned until sentencing at 0900 hours tomorrow."

Thank God for that. Another minute of hearing the condemnation of Spiteri would be enough to put me to sleep.

He got back to his room at the hotel and found a message waiting for him. It simply said, 'Contact General White immediately'.

Great.

He put the call through, and once again the General was ready and waiting to accept it.

"Colonel Taylor, was I not absolutely clear that you were to stay put in Paris, keep your head down, and wait for everything to blow over?"

"Yes, Sir."

"Was I not absolutely clear that you had to stay out of the news?"

"Yes, Sir."

"Then please explain to me why you not only went to North Africa, but ended up in a fight with protestors, and a key witness in an UEN tribunal of a senior officer?"

"Sir, I was only trying to do what's best for everyone."

"What's best!" he screamed, "You are an officer in the United States Marine Corps, and therefore you belong to me!"

"Maybe I used to be, Sir, but I'm not the combat officer I signed up to be. I'm a puppet being flown around the World for entertainment."

"You're whatever the Corps wants you to be, Taylor. Now, I've let a lot slide because of the great things you've done for us all, but this has to stop. You're running around like a cowboy out there raising all kinds of hell. I'm told you are needed in court tomorrow for the sentencing of Lieutenant Colonel Spiteri. After that, you are to return immediately and report here, where you will be dealt with accordingly!"

"Yes, Sir."

The General shook his head, "What happened to you, Taylor? In war, you were one of the greatest assets the World had, and now you're nothing but a troublemaker. I don't want to hear your name on any channel, whether it's civilian or military, for some time. Do not screw up again!"

The transmission stopped, and Taylor was left feeling nothing but pissed off. He turned to see Jafar had watched the whole thing from the other side of the room.

"What does he want of you?"

"Who knows? All I know is life was a lot simpler when we were at war."

"But you said you didn't like war."

"Maybe I was wrong. Anyway, we're stuck here till tomorrow now. I hate to say it, but let's keep our heads down. Wherever we go, we seem to attract trouble. We can't find trouble if we stay here. I'll order up room service, and we'll have a few drinks."

Taylor spent the rest of the afternoon flicking through channels on the TV, the thing most guaranteed to bore Jafar to death. At 2000 he ordered up food and was surprised to see it arrive within ten minutes. A staff member pushed a trolley through into their room. It was the best thing he'd seen all day, and the only thing he'd been looking forward to. As the man lifted off the covers from their meal, the lights went out.

"Ah, hell."

It was a complete blackout.

"Don't worry, Monsieur, the secondary power will start shortly."

Nothing happened. As Taylor's eyes adjusted to the dark, he stepped out into the corridor. The whole building was out. He went back to the room and hit the switch for the window shutters to open, but the power outage meant they wouldn't move. He pulled the manual cord override, and they slid aside.

The city before them was still lit up as before.

"I don't understand it," said the concierge.

"You've not had this kind of power outage before?"

"Oh, yes, but the whole block, not just this hotel, and it recovers within fifteen seconds."

Taylor strode back to the wardrobe and pulled on his Reitech suit.

"What do you think is happening?" Jafar asked, who seemed surprised at his response.

"I'm not sure, but I don't like it."

He could see Jafar had no concept of the scenario they might be facing, but he was automatically suspicious. He heard footsteps in the corridor and quickly grabbed his pistol, heading to the door to look out. The shadow of a man with a gun was approaching. Taylor leaned out just far enough not to be noticed by the figure until he was right on him.

He grabbed the man's arm and pulled him inside the room. He was in utter shock, but Taylor's firm grasp had him pinned and with a pistol to his head. It was one of the UEN Military policemen who had escorted him to the court that morning. Taylor relaxed his grip and took a step back.

"What's going on here?"

"No idea, Sir. The power is out. Communications are being jammed. I really must continue, Sir."

Taylor took his hand off him, and the man instantly leapt out the door. He turned back to see the concierge was terrified. Before any of them could say a word, they heard something tumble to the ground in the corridor in the direction the soldier had gone. Mitch leaned out the doorway to look and saw the soldier collapsed and lifeless. He turned to see several armed figures moving towards him. They had already noticed his head, despite the near darkness.

As he ducked back, a dart struck the doorframe. He spun back against the wall and threw the concierge aside to get him out of the way. Jafar also had his pistol drawn. They were the only weapons they had. Seconds later, the first gunman rushed through the doorway with his rifle

145

held high. Taylor let him pass and went at the second man through the door. He smashed his fist into the man's face. As the punch connected, he noticed a night vision visor hanging down from a compact helmet.

As the man tumbled back into the next gunman, he saw they all wore Reitech suits. Jafar launched out from the bathroom area to tackle the first man who had come through the door, shoving him across the room so that he smashed through one of the interior walls and landed in the bedroom. The third gunman got a shot off, and the dart hit Taylor in the chest, embedding in his armour. Jafar responded by firing two shots at his attacker, but the thick armour he wore absorbed both.

Distracted from taking another shot, Taylor took the opportunity to smack the man in the face with his pistol. He collapsed unconscious to the floor. Jafar rushed through to the bedroom and hauled the man out, who was dazed but still conscious. Taylor yanked the dart out from his armour and looked at it with surprise and intrigue.

"What do you suppose are in them, Jafar?"

The alien reached over and took it from his hands, jamming it into the throat of the man he was holding. He went limp immediately in his hand.

"What did you do that for?"

He stepped up to the body and felt for a pulse. It was still there.

"It's not lethal, but you didn't know that beforehand."

Jafar had nothing to say on the subject. Taylor took off the man's helmet and pulled it on to his head. The night vision gave him a near perfect view of everything around. He looked down and quickly studied everything on the man.

"French Special Forces. Can't be."

"Why?"

"Because it's crazy, Jafar."

He thought back over the day's events.

"Oh, no, the Spanish going after the camps tomorrow; Spiteri is probably a hero for the Earth for Humans campaign. Him being forced to kill protestors because of the UEN, when he actively supports the execution of the aliens. The conflict within him is something they can cling to, and rally more people to their cause."

Jafar looked completely confused by the hypothesis.

It seemed farfetched and bizarre, so much so, it made a little sense to Taylor.

"Spiteri is the perfect man to highlight the stupidity and absurdity of keeping the Krys alive. They're here to rescue him before sentencing."

Taylor still couldn't believe the French President could be in on it, but he knew plenty of those around him would be capable of it.

"Come on, we have to stop this, and make sure Spiteri gets to that sentencing tomorrow, or he'll be a catalyst for war in Europe."

They each took one of the rifles from the incapacitated Frenchmen and rushed out the door, leaving only the hotel concierge still backed up against one of the walls and frozen stiff in fear.

Taylor was at a jogging pace now, going as fast as he could safely do so when he had no idea how many other gunmen occupied the building.

Two marines against God knows how many well training and armed gunmen? Great odds.

The elevators were clearly down, so they headed for the stairs. The door was almost jammed shut and appeared not to have been opened in years. The steps before them were covered in dust. Clearly, they had become completely dependant on the elevators and the expectation they would never fail.

Footsteps thundered down on the stairs from above, most likely another wave of the gunmen they had heard before.

"Where is Spiteri?"

"Two floors above us," Jafar replied.

"How does the shit seem to follow us wherever we go?" he muttered, as they stormed up the stairs.

Taylor was in the dark, just as he had been during the war. No comms, no technology to aid in enemy troop movements. Just him, a gun, and his friends; or single friend, as was the case here. They flew up the two flights of stairs at lightning speed, twenty seconds ahead of those coming down from the roof.

They both knew they had to deal with those approaching before going any further. They took up positions either side of the corridor, continuing on five metres to a turn that would provide some cover. Then they readied themselves. The troops rushed into the corridor as if there were no threat at all. Taylor could only assume they had seen him and assumed he was one of them, due to his equipment; a single lucky break at least.

He squeezed the trigger, and the dart hit the throat of the first while Jafar's shot went into the cheek of another. Their two comrades were through the door before they had realised the danger, due to the silent weaponry. They took them down the same way as the first. For a moment they stayed put, waiting for more to come through, but that was the last of them.

Taylor got back up to his feet and pointed for Jafar to go on and lead the way. He knew the location of Spiteri better than he did. As they passed quickly down the corridors, they took a bend and found two gunmen at a doorway and another rushing out with Spiteri at his side. They saw Jafar, and the game was up. Darts soared down the corridor, forcing them to duck back down.

"Shit," muttered Taylor, "Come on, they must be going for the roof via the other stairs."

Taylor rushed back to where they had taken down the four Frenchmen and hit the stairs as quickly as he could.

"We have to get there before they do, or we're finished."

Taylor was at the front when they burst onto the rooftop, stopping instantly as they were met by the sight of Armand with a pistol to his head.

"Lay down your weapons, or he dies!"

Taylor didn't know what to do for a moment and looked around for some other possibility. Another dozen French Special Forces occupied the roof, with two transports ready to whisk them away.

"Lay down your weapons, and you will not be harmed!"

"Do it," said Taylor.

Jafar seemed utterly astonished.

"They don't mean to hurt us. They don't want any blood spilled here."

He put the rifle down, and Jafar reluctantly followed suit.

"You're sidearms, too!"

Taylor drew out his pistol and put it down before him. As he stood back up, he felt naked. Not a single weapon to hand and helpless to stop them taking Spiteri. Several of the troops rushed past them and down the stairs. It was clear they wanted to recover their wounded. He wasn't sure if it were evidence they were concerned with, or leaving their comrades behind.

"Thank you for trying!" Armand shouted.

Spiteri strode over to them under the cover of the soldiers and had a broad smile about his face.

"I think you picked the wrong side, Colonel."

"I wasn't aware we had any amongst humans."

"Then you're an idiot. Look around you. The only time we were unified was when we were at war. It can't survive during peacetime."

"They'll just parade you around as a poster boy for all that's wrong in the World."

"Then let them, for I'll be playing my part in doing what should have been done four years ago. Genocide isn't a pretty business, but someone has to do it."

"Maybe they do have to die or be exiled or something, but this isn't the way! We can't turn on one another while the threat remains very real. What happens when the next invasion comes and humanity is divided?"

"Then we should be sure to root out alien sympathisers and enablers quickly, and you are one of them, aren't you. Colonel?" he said, walking over to Jafar and staring at the alien.

"I don't know what your game is, but I don't like it, and letting you stand by his side was Taylor's biggest mistake, and probably his undoing. You've lost, Colonel. You've let the enemy in. They have manipulated you, and now you let them stand beside you as equal."

Taylor could see his point of view, even if he knew he was wrong about Jafar.

The French were quick to recover their comrades; a task made easy by the power of the Reitech suits that allowed a soldier to carry another without any restriction at all.

Spiteri picked up Taylor's pistol from the floor and pointed it at Jafar's head. Taylor knew it was helpless to act, but Armand leapt in to try.

"You don't want to spill blood here, Colonel!"

He turned around in shock.

"No? Really? Why would I not want to kill one alien, when I am happy to kill them all?"

"This can still be resolved peacefully. And even if the powers of the World agree to genocide, they'll never condemn that one. He has been invaluable to us."

"Probably because he's working an angle! Getting at us from within."

The Frenchman who had the gun to Armand's head stepped forward to resolve the matter.

"No blood is to be spilled here!"

"But…"

"I have strict orders. We are to accomplish this mission, only if it can be done without any fatalities on either side. You will put the weapon down and come with us!"

Spiteri waved the gun around a bit with a smile, just to prove he had Jafar's life in his hands before finally laying it down a couple of metres from Taylor.

"You should come with us, Taylor. A man like you should be on the right side. Leave this creature behind with his own kind and continue the fight you excel at.

"You know I can't do that."

"Why, because you swore an oath to some idiots, some of whom have put you behind bars, others have thrown you into an arena to slug it out with creatures that could rip you apart. Choose the right side before it's too late, Taylor."

He was helpless to act now and could only hope they'd make it out alive. Finally, the Frenchman ordered them all to load up. He dragged Armand across the rooftop to the entrance to his ship. At the last moment when all were aboard, he pushed the man forward to quickly shut the door.

Taylor and Jafar leapt for their handguns and took aim, but the craft was already lifting off the rooftop as they took aim. They looked to Armand for answers. He seemed surprisingly calm, despite the drama.

"Guess there'll be no sentencing tomorrow?" asked Taylor.

"Never mind, we have larger problems now."

"Ain't that the truth?"

With his last word, the power to the building came back on. The three of them ambled back to Taylor's room. The door was still open, and the entrance trashed from the fight. The only thing missing was the concierge who must have finally mustered the courage to leave.

"So what now?"

"Negotiations are still ongoing at the UEN, but with several key members missing. I should imagine all attempts are being made to get the Spanish back to the table. Now we wait and see if they really do cross over the sea and make their attempt at the prisons."

"And we just let them? There are German soldiers defending those prisons now. Will we let two European, two human powers slug it out over this?"

"I don't think we have a choice."

Taylor turned to Jafar, "What's your take on all this?"

"You are making a simple situation complicated."

"And, what would you do?"

"Put them to work or put them to death."

"Hardly humane, is it?" asked Armand.

"Is civil war?" retorted Taylor.

"So now it's a waiting game? Waiting for what could be the start of a war between major powers, the likes we have not seen in a few hundred years? Have we not fought enough recently?"

"You like war though?" asked Jafar.

Taylor turned and looked pained, already wishing he hadn't made those comments.

"I didn't say I liked war. I said it wasn't all bad, and some elements were preferable to the life I now had to lead. And anyway, I was talking about war with the Krys, not other human beings."

It seemed Jafar couldn't tell the difference, but he nodded in acceptance.

CHAPTER SEVEN

0900 hours.

Taylor had barely slept waiting for the news. He'd been expecting a call from General White all night. He'd done his utmost to stay out of trouble, but it had found him that night, and yet, no call came.

Every news agency was focused on the gathering of Spanish forces and awaiting their next move. Five seconds past the hour, and nothing had happened. Taylor prayed for a moment that it had all been a sabre-rattling exercise, but then it started.

"We're getting reports that the thousands of soldiers are boarding craft ready to cross the sea as the President warned. This is it."

"Christ, Europe could be at war in a matter of hours, and what the hell can we do about it?"

Just as he said it, a message came through that

interrupted the news. He accepted it and was pleased to see Captain Ryan before him.

"Sir, glad to see you're all right, but damn, what the hell are you doing in Brussels? General White is livid and is after your balls."

"Yeah, well, he can wait in line. We have larger problems. Where are you?"

"On our way. We'll be putting down at a landing zone one click south of your hotel. I am ordered to recover you and Jafar immediately, and return you to report directly to General White."

"Yeah, well you can pick us up, but I'm not leaving Europe while there is still a chance we can make a difference."

"Sir, I am under strict orders."

"Do you not trust me, Captain? I knew I could always depend on Captain Reyes and his crew, and you have honoured him, will you sway from that path now?"

He shook his head. Taylor knew he had persuaded the man who had long called Taylor a friend.

"Sir, no matter what you do, the shit seems to slide off you. Can you extend that luxury to us when we get home?"

"I wouldn't worry about getting home, Captain. We've got a war to stop."

"One last thing, Sir. Just moments before I called, Tsengal woke up."

"What? Is he talking?"

"Not yet, but his eyes are open, and something's going on in there."

It was the best news he had heard in a long time.

"Thank you, Captain. We'll be there when you land."

As the message ended, Armand stepped through into the room.

"My ship is en route, will you join us?"

He looked unsure, but Taylor continued in an excited manner.

"I have aboard a friend of Jafar. He's the only survivor from Red 1. I have long believed he may hold some vital information for us. Before he slipped into a coma, he tried to tell me something important, who knows what."

That seemed to get his attention.

"Of course, Colonel. If I may, I will have my personal staff transfer over to your ship where we can work from."

Taylor was surprised at his enthusiasm, but it gave him a great excuse for not obeying White's orders. Taylor couldn't wait to see Tsengal, and it seemed forever that they stood at the landing pad awaiting the ship. Finally, the sight of it made Taylor feel the best he had done in days. The Deveron was an eternal sign of hope for the Colonel.

Captain Ryan came out to greet them in person, but Taylor did not stop for any pleasantries. He rushed inside and towards the room where he knew Tsengal would be. Jafar was close at his side but didn't seem to share his enthusiasm.

"Have you not looked forward to this moment for all these years?"

"Yes."

"Well, you don't look it. Four years he's been dead to the World and is now awake."

"I always expected him to wake up, and I could wait as long as need be."

"Yeah, well, I'm not that patient."

He rushed into the room to see the ship's Doctor at his side monitoring levels. Tsengal turned his head just a little to acknowledge their arrival and seemed to recognise the two of them.

"My God, you really have woken up. It's good to see you back from the dead."

Tsengal did nothing but nod in recognition.

"You must have so many questions, as do we. Important thing to know is that we won the war."

"He needs rest," said the Doctor.

"Any chance of him speaking anytime soon?"

"His body seems to be coming online fairly rapidly. He could well be talking within a few minutes or a few hours. It'll be quite some time before he walks again."

"You let me know the second he shows any sign of improving. I want to know what he knows. God knows what he saw in the time he was away."

He left the room feeling the best he had in a while.

"The World maybe going to shit, but we're coming back together," he whispered.

Armand stood waiting outside the room. He had with him three assistants and two bodyguards. It appeared the wounded man had already been replaced.

"Step this way."

He led them through to the operations room where he imagined they would be spending many days, but right now the most important thing was the news. He turned it on to see a live feed of ships landing in North Africa.

"They're really doing it?" he asked.

"It was inevitable they would cross the water. The only question is are they willing to fire on the Germans?"

"What do you think?"

"Doesn't matter what I think, only what we can affect."

"How long do we have until all this kicks off?"

"Protestors will move out of their way. Having soldiers rolling in willing to kill every Kry in the land is exactly what they have been calling for. It'll take them an hour to get assembled and in place ready to assault. Then the only question is how much are they willing to negotiate with the German forces there before they go in?"

"How long would you give them?"

"I wouldn't set an ultimatum on allied forces. We shouldn't be killing our own. But I guess they'll give the Germans a thirty-minute ultimatum to think it over. Anymore than that, and they risk other forces being moved into play."

"You're a smart man, Colonel."

"Smart enough to have stayed alive this long, so what's our play here? We heading over to negotiate with the Spanish forces in person? I know a few among them. I might be able to sway a few senior officers."

"No, we tried going to the source once and look how that went. We're sitting this one out for now. The UEN will call upon us when they need us."

"Shit, the World's going to hell, and you want us to sit tight and watch? I'm not too good at that."

"Even so, that is our job. There are forces at play here far larger than either one of us."

"That's what worries me."

Taylor got up and left, for there was nothing more to say on the matter. He strode up the bridge where the crew sat idle.

"Your orders, Sir? Where are we heading?"

"Absolutely no where," he said with a sigh.

"What? World's going to hell and we aren't heading for it? Colonel Taylor isn't heading for it? What's happened?"

"Can't say I like it either, but this isn't our fight. If the Spanish and the Germans really want to kill each other because of a few Mechs, who are we to stop them?"

"Somebody has to."

"This isn't our fight, Captain! We are members of the United States armed forces! We have zero authority in these lands!"

"Amazing how they were happy to have us when aliens were crawling through every street."

The bridge went silent. None of them liked sitting there while the World seemingly went to hell again. Taylor knew he had to raise morale, something to break through the thick and depressing atmosphere that had arisen. He stood up tall and proud.

"I know what you are all feeling, because believe me I feel exactly the same. It makes me sick to the stomach what is going on right now. But don't forget what we got through together these past few years. Nobody ever said life was gonna be some paradise once we beat the invasion. We stick together, survive, and do our duty to our country, the Corps, and our race, and we'll be just fine!"

It sounded uplifting. He wasn't sure he believed it, but at least the rest of them did. Just when they expected him to continue, a call came through from the Doc.

"Sir, Tsengal is coming to."

"Thank you, Doctor."

He looked back up to the crew. "You see that. One who was lost to us has returned and is making a recovery. That's hope if I ever saw it."

He raced off the bridge to reach Tsengal. As he got to the entrance to the room, Armand met him.

"What can I do for you, Councillor?"

"I hear your friend is awake. If what you tell me about

him is true, I'd love to meet him and see what he has to say."

Taylor nodded in agreement. He didn't even think about it. All he cared about was seeing his friend was okay. He entered the room to see in his eyes that his mind was returning to him, and that was a great relief.

"Great to meet you," added Armand.

Tsengal turned his attention to the Councillor, and Taylor noticed an odd expression on the alien's face, almost as if he recognised the man but could not understand how. It was something for a later conversation in private.

"Great to see you again, buddy. We were all wondering if you'd ever wake up. It's been four years."

He was silent, clearly trying to piece together his memories.

"Last time I saw you, Tsengal, sounded like you had something real important to tell me. You remember what that was?"

He was racking his mind for the memory, but it wasn't coming to him.

"It may take some time before his memory fully recovers, and he may still have blank spots for awhile, maybe permanently," added the Doctor, "He should get some more rest."

"Councillor, can you give us a moment?"

"Sure, Colonel."

Something was eating at Taylor that he had to ask. The

second Armand was out the room; he came right out with it.

"You recognised him, didn't you? How and from where?"

Armand was just the other side of the door and listening in. He was as eager to know the answer as Taylor was. Tsengal was still racking his brain for answers, but he could find none. He shook his head.

"It's okay. You get some rest and tell me anything you can, when you can."

Armand was long gone by the time Taylor stepped out of the room. He returned to the operations room and found Armand sat there as if he had never moved. He had no real reason to assume otherwise.

They were watching the news and were absolutely fixated on it.

"Guys, this sucks. We can't just stand here helplessly watching this unfold," Taylor murmured.

His words fell on deaf ears, as they all knew they had to do exactly that. The Spanish troops were formed up and ready to move at any moment. Reporters were at the scene of several prisons, waiting to film the scenes of carnage that may ensue. But then the news network went back to the studio with an important message.

"President Marin of Spain is about to make a statement from Madrid, live in..."

The video cut immediately to the announcement, and

Taylor noticed the French President stood at his side, along with several other European leaders. Captain Ryan walked into the room just in time to see it.

"This can't be good," whispered Taylor.

"They calling it all off?" asked Ryan.

Nobody could bear to answer him, as they watched and dreaded what might come next.

"In light of the recent inactions of the UEN and the ongoing threat of the alien populace on earth, Spain can no longer remain as a member of an organisation which actively defends the existence of an invading force on our very doorstep. And we are not alone. From this day forth, Spain is withdrawing from the UEN, along with six other nations who have already agreed to be part of a new initiative, a new organisation; one which has the safety of European citizens at its heart."

"They're setting up the crowds for civil war in Europe."

"Surely not, Colonel?" asked Ryan.

They watched open mouthed as the speech continued.

"In partnership with my good friend and colleague, President Jacques, I want to announce the creation of the European Alliance, an Alliance of free nations without universal rule or regulation, with the single aim of making the World safe for all. I want to extend a welcome to all our European brothers and sisters. Join us, for the greater good."

There was a long pause, but no one in the audience

made as much as a sound. They waited with bated breath to hear it to the end.

"May all Europeans see the way to peace and security for us all, and join us in this venture which will finally bring an end to the wars which have plagued our nations. As we speak, the armies of Spain are poised to move against the remaining aliens on Earth, and while I would never wish harm to come to another human, any who stand in the way of this task will meet the same fate. The advance begins in precisely ten minutes. All human forces protecting alien life have until that time to walk free. We do not ask that you lay down your weapons, nor surrender. For you are our allies. Simply join us, or walk free. Thank you, and good luck to you all."

"Ten minutes!" Ryan sighed. "That's a hell of an ultimatum. Surely they won't go ahead with it."

It was a waiting game now. Five minutes later, the news attention was turned to a hastily set up conference led by the German Prime Minster, Ms Muller, in Brussels where she had remained for the trial. She stood confidently and looked firm, but they could see in her eyes the sadness of what she was expecting.

"Thank you all for coming. I am sure you all appreciate the seriousness of the unfolding events in the World. On behalf of the UEN, I am forced to condemn the departure of nations from the UEN. Since 1957, the powers of Europe have stood as one, just as they did during the most recent wars. However, the UEN respects the rights and freedoms of those nations who choose to depart the Union. Additionally, I must state in no uncertain terms, that the UEN will not be bullied, nor stand down from its duties."

She took a deep breath before she continued with what none of them wanted to hear.

"The warmongering of this new Alliance will not be tolerated. The UEN policy on prisoners of war remains as it always has, and the forces of all our nations will fight to protect those laws and policies. The UEN does not seek bloodshed on either side, and will only respond in kind. I must repeat the comments of many of my colleagues in the UEN that we do not want war. Do not bring it upon us."

This isn't right, Taylor thought.

He could not believe they had reached the current situation so quickly, and it was clear it stunned all around him, except for Armand. The Councillor seemed all too comfortable with the events as they unfolded. He wondered if maybe he really just was that cold and heartless, or if he had a vested interest in a new conflict. He put the thought aside, as it didn't make any sense. Muller was rounding off her speech. It was heartfelt, but he couldn't imagine it would be enough to sway minds that were already polarised.

"I must underline once again. The UEN does not wish

pain and suffering to come to a single human being nor alien. Remember what we fought for, and remember how hard won this peace was. Thank you, and may God be with us all."

God? He ain't gonna save you.

He looked at his watch. They were two minutes from the ultimatum. The news cameras were on the Spanish forces once again, with a timer ticking loudly at the corner of the screen. They cut to the German defenders who were equally as anxious.

"Surely they won't fight? Not to defend the Krys?" Ryan whispered.

Taylor shrugged. He prayed they would open the gates and leave the Spaniards to it. It was now the only possibility he could see for peace. The timer kept creeping down, and neither side seemed willing to back down.

Come on, don't do it.

The timer reached zero and for a moment nothing happened at all. They all held their breath and hoped, but it was not to be. After a few seconds, the Spanish forces launched into action.

Armoured vehicles rolled across the sands towards the prison complex. It was the Gafsa compound they were seeing where Taylor had recently been. They watched in silence as the vehicles tore across the sands. The press crews were filming from the air a kilometre away.

The armoured vehicles were only half a kilometre

away now, and they could only watch in horror as the guns opened fire, tearing holes in the gates and walls of the facility. The troops at the walls returned fire, but they could do little against the might of the army bearing down on them. As the vehicles reached the walls and smashed into the compound, a dust cloud arose so high the camera crews could no longer see what was unfolding.

"They really did it? Human versus human?"

"It sucks, Captain, but that's our lives now. What do we do about it?" Taylor asked.

They looked to Armand for answers.

"The UEN will not and cannot stand by and let this go unanswered."

Taylor could see he knew a lot more than he was letting on as he pointed to the news screen.

The cameras panned up to the skies to dozens of fighters flashing past the news copter and opening fire. They panned back from the prison to the rest of the incoming Spanish forces. Explosions erupted amongst their ranks, and the fire demolished armoured vehicles.

Anti-aircraft missiles and gunfire soared into the sky. A few seconds later, the cameras rocked aboard the news copter as a massive explosion burst through the ship.

"We've been hit. We've been hit!" the screams rang out as the cameras shook. "We're going down!"

Screams followed until the screens went dead, and the news feed cut back to an anchorman in an office far from the action. He was too stunned to speak for a full ten seconds."

"I...we apologise, for we have lost the feed there in Tunisia and are experiencing technical difficulties..."

He looked down at new reports coming in at the screen in front of him.

"We are getting confirmed reports that UEN forces have engaged the Spanish armies in North Africa, in what seems to be a bitter battle fought over the multiple prisons in the north of the continent."

"What he hell do we do?" Ryan asked.

"Right now? Nothing we can do."

"Why? They're killing each other."

"Yes, and what is America's position on this?"

He shrugged his shoulders.

"Precisely, this isn't the last war. That was total war where every human being fought on whatever front he or she happened to be on. But this is something very different."

"So, we do nothing because we aren't from here?"

"That about sums it up."

Taylor got to his feet. He'd seen enough. He left the room and headed for Tsengal. The alien was happy to see him, although he was surprised to not find Jafar there. Ryan stepped through a moment later.

"Jafar, where is he?"

"On guard at our perimeter with three of the crew," he

replied. "World's going to hell. We hold two aliens and a UEN Councillor on board, think we aren't a target? No, I want to be ready when someone comes after us."

"A wise move," he said, looking back to Tsengal. A screen was on near him, and he was looking through recent history since the war had ended.

"Memory coming back much?"

"Yes."

"That man who was in here earlier, you recognised him, didn't you?"

"I think so."

Taylor tapped a few buttons on the screen and brought up Armand's profile with a picture of him.

"How? How do you know him?"

Tsengal seemed to study the face very carefully until finally something clicked in his mind. His eyes widened in horror.

"What is it?"

Tsengal's memories were flooding back to him, and the subject he so desperately needed to tell Taylor. He didn't know where to begin, but Armand's face was what was stuck in his mind, and he was beginning to remember why.

"What we discovered on Red 1. That is the reason I had to get back you. Colonel Chandra ordered me to do so."

"Okay, well, spit it out."

"Hundreds of thousands of humans in incubation chambers, like you saw before in the war. Maybe even millions of them."

"And Chandra discovered this?"

"Yes, deep below the surface."

"Well, where did they come from? What, clones or what?"

"We did not have time to find out. But what I know for certain is that Councillor; he is one of them. He was one of the faces I saw there."

"Maybe a million humans, and you remember his face? How can you be sure?"

"It was him; I was as close to him as you are to me now."

"So these humans are somehow working for the Krys?"

"Why else would they be there?"

"This is crazy. I can't believe what I'm hearing," Ryan said.

He waited while Taylor tried to make sense of what they had heard.

"You are one hundred percent about this?"

"I spent years trying to get back to you with this news which would have died with the Colonel."

Taylor sighed; the idea was quite simply frightening. Unfortunately, it was starting to make sense.

"You're not believing this? It's crazy."

"Sounds crazy, Ryan, maybe. I wish it was crazy, yes, but it's starting to make sense. Chandra and I came across a number of incubated humans during the war. Something none of us could ever explain, and every time we recovered any of them, the evidence was destroyed instantly. It's the reason Ramstein was flattened, or we think anyway."

"So let me get this straight. What you're telling me is that the human race has been infiltrated by other humans, programmed or created somehow by the enemy, to penetrate deep within our political system and do what?"

"Maybe to do exactly what we are seeing today. Armies who were recently the strongest of allies are now at each other's throats. This fighting is not going to stop anytime soon."

"But why?"

Ryan looked to Tsengal for answers, but he did not have any.

"Divide and conquer," stated Taylor. "The Krys threw everything they had at us, sheer mass of numbers, superior technology, and Planet Killing weapons. But what beat them? The strength of humanity united under one banner."

"Okay, let's say you're right. They do what? Push all sides into war and then sit back while we slug it out, weaken each other to the point where they can come back and triumph over..." He shook his head, "Oh, shit, it really is working."

"What proof do you have of this?"

"None, only what I saw."

"We have to get this information out there. People are

killing each other over this," said Ryan.

"And how do you propose we do that?"

He began to open his mouth and then stopped, realising the situation they were in. Tsengal suddenly spasmed and then spat out blood over himself. He began shaking violently.

"Doctor!" yelled Taylor.

The man rushed in to his aid but looked completely clueless as to what was happening. Tsengal flat lined and went still. The doctor was pushing needles into him and pulled down a hinged device from the ceiling, placing it over Tsengal's heart. His body spasmed again as electricity pulsed through his body in an attempt to revive him.

"No, we can't lose him now. Save him!" Taylor begged.

The Doctor was trying everything, but to no avail, and then he stopped.

"What are you giving up for?" screamed Taylor.

"I am sorry, Colonel, but he's gone."

"Gone? He just recovered!"

"I don't understand it, something has shocked his body, but I can't see how."

"Well find out!"

He was looking over everything until finally he checked the nutritional drip that led into his body. He opened up the container the line was drawing from and recoiled at the smell.

"What is it?"

"Not that I know for certain, but I'd say he's been poisoned with something truly nasty. If it is what I'm thinking, he didn't stand a chance."

Taylor turned to Ryan with sheer hatred in his eyes.

"Get guards on Armand now!"

"Sir, he's an UEN Councillor. What if we're wrong?"

Taylor simply glared back at him until he did as ordered.

"All right, but this is on you."

It was obvious Ryan had a hard time believing the facts they had been presented with, but that was no surprise to Taylor. They were as bad as news could expect to be. Taylor heard shouts down the corridor and more over his comms channel. He rushed out of the room. Ryan was at the end of the corridor attending to an unconscious crewmember.

An alarm sounded throughout the ship as he rushed to the Captain.

"Where is Armand?"

"They've gone. We've got two wounded."

Taylor drew his pistol and rushed for the ramp out of the ship. He found Jafar and the other crew with their weapons at the ready but utterly unaware of what the emergency was.

"Where's Armand?"

"Departed by car about thirty seconds ago, Sir!"

"Fuck!" he screamed.

"What are your orders, Sir?"

"You stay put. Be extra vigilant, and report and all suspicious activity. Councillor Armand is to be considered an enemy agent from now on!"

They all looked confused but did as ordered. He paced up to Jafar so he could talk more privately, but he did not attempt to break the news softly.

"Tsengal is dead. Killed by that coward Armand. He's one of the clones, or reprogrammed humans, whatever they are. Like we saw back in the war. Tsengal confirmed it and was killed because of it."

"Then his duty has been done."

Taylor seemed surprised by the comment.

"How so?"

"His last orders were to return to you with news of what he had seen. He accomplished that, did he not?"

"Well, yeah."

"Then his death was not in vain and his mission accomplished."

Mitch got what he meant, but it didn't make him any less angry about the situation. He rushed back aboard the ship. Ryan was awaiting him at the top of the ramp.

"Casualties?"

"Two wounded. They'll be okay."

"Everything that Tsengal told us before he died, you have records of?"

He shook his head.

"Armand had our surveillance and recording drives

fried before he left. Onboard cameras are still in operation, but they're not recording anything they see."

"So we've got no evidence of either Tsengal's report, or of Armand's escape and assault on the crew?"

He shook his head once again.

"This is turning from shit to worse, Captain. Tell me you have some good news."

"I wish I did, Sir."

He stopped for a moment, trying to think who he could go to with the news. He knew he had no choice but to go to General White, the commanding officer who wanted to hear nothing more from him for years to come.

"Come with me, Captain. We need to talk to White."

"Why me, Sir?"

"Because besides me, you're the only one who heard Tsengal's story, and you think he'll take my word for it?"

They stepped into Taylor's personal quarters and put the call through. The General's secretary answered.

"Put me through to the General," he commanded.

"I'm sorry, but the General is otherwise engaged."

"The World is going to shit, and we might just have some information which could save it, so put me through to the fucking General!" he screamed.

The officer seemed taken aback by the response, but like many on the base, he knew Taylor's reputation and found it hard to say no.

"All right, Colonel, transferring you now."

The General appeared before him and looked flustered.

"What the hell do you want, Colonel? Haven't you caused enough trouble?"

"Tsengal, Sir, he woke up and has revealed some vital new information."

"This better be good, Taylor. I'm a busy man."

"It'll blow your mind."

He had the General's attention now.

"Taylor, you've got my attention."

"You remember the human incubation chambers we found during the wars, Sir?"

"I heard about them, never did manage to get any looked at by experts."

"No, because the enemy had them destroyed before we could learn the truth. Red 1, where Colonel Chandra and Tsengal were left; deep underground they found God knows how many humans like that, maybe millions."

"Wait, wait, wait. Just hold up there, Colonel. You're telling me in alien space, on the alien planet, Chandra discovered these humans?"

"Yes, Sir. I'm still no closer to understanding if they're some kind of test tube creations or reprogrammed prisoners from the first war or what, but what I do know is that at least one now walks among us on Earth, confirmed by Tsengal with his own eyes."

White still seemed baffled by the whole thing.

"This is all sounding like crazy talk, Colonel. Get to the

punch line."

"Sir, they're infiltrating governments, starting wars, weakening humanity from within. Councillor Armand is one of them, and is just one at the heart of it in the UEN. I bet the US government has these spies embedded, too."

"Why am I only just hearing about this now, and from you? These are big claims, Colonel. You better be able to back them up. I want Tsengal returned immediately for questioning by our top people here Stateside."

"He's dead, Sir."

"He's what?"

"Murdered by Armand and his people before they managed to slip off this ship."

"What other evidence do you have besides your word?"

"Mine, Sir," Captain Ryan stated.

"Great, one of Taylor's fan club ain't gonna cut it. What do you have that is real, that can prove this, that will convince anyone this crazy story is true?"

"Nothing," he replied with a sigh.

"Then it is nothing; hearsay, scuttlebutt, and a waste of my goddamn time. The World is in real trouble, Colonel. We need real solutions. Get your ass back here immediately, and forget all this nonsense until such time as you have some actual proof. Get your head screwed on, Taylor. We may well need your skills in the days and months to come."

The transmission cut out, and the two of them were

left speechless.

"So that's it? We can't prove it, so he won't believe us?" asked Ryan.

"Does seem pretty farfetched until you have seen all we have seen."

"Then what now? We can't go home and forget all this?"

"No, we'll just have to find another way."

CHAPTER EIGHT

"It is the second day of fighting at the Gafsa prison, and Spanish forces now occupy the northern sector and claim to have executed up to fifteen hundred alien prisoners. Meanwhile UEN forces continue to gain in number and dig into their positions. Casualties on both sides are now numbering in the hundreds, and there seems little hope for a ceasefire."

Taylor, Jafar, and Ryan sat around the conference table fixated on the news. They had talked most of the night over what to do with the information they had and still not come up with an answer.

"You think Armand will come gunning for us?" asked Ryan.

"No, not yet. Right now we're a US vessel on peacetime operations. He can't touch us. At least not until we go after him."

"So what now, then?"

"We need to find someone who will listen to us. Someone who can spread the word."

"Who do we know who we can trust?"

"Those who fought with us in the wars," he replied.

"Like who?"

"We'll start with Dupont."

"I thought the guy hated you and you hated him right back?"

"Yeah, but when you start running out of friends..."

He put the call through, and Dupont answered personally. He clearly knew who was calling and smiled as he answered. It was a slightly sleazy smirk. Taylor didn't know how to take the man anymore. He seemed to have humanity's interests at heart, but they simply rarely got on.

"Colonel Taylor, you must be in some real trouble to be calling on me?"

"You got it, General. You know how the World is turning, and I know it was your boys who took Spiteri."

"Come on, Colonel, that's a little farfetched."

"I know because I was there. I saw their uniforms and tussled with them personally."

His face turned from a smile, realising Taylor wasn't bluffing.

"But I don't care about any of that. What I care about is stopping this damn war before it blows up in all our faces."

"That's out of my hands. France wants the aliens dead, and nobody should stand in her way."

"Not at any cost?"

"You've obviously got something to say, so get on with it, Colonel."

He took a deep breath and tried to find a way of making it sound believable.

"We have reason to believe alien programmed or cloned humans have infiltrated governments, certainly in Europe, and probably elsewhere, and are pushing all sides to war, in an attempt to destabilise the World ready for another attack."

Dupont burst out into laughter, and Taylor didn't blame him. It did sound absurd when there was no first-hand account or evidence backing it up.

"Colonel, I'm glad to see you still have a sense of humour, but I really do have work to do. Thank you for the entertainment, though," he replied and ended the call.

"Figures," said Taylor. "I guess if we can't convince one side, we'll just have to work the other."

He put a call through to General Schulz and was met by one of his staff he did not recognise.

"Please put me through to General Schulz. I have important news."

"I am sorry, but the General is extremely busy."

"I'm not wasting anyone's time here. It is vital I am put through to the General."

"The fact you got through to his office at all is only a courtesy due to who you are, but any information you have can be relayed when the General has time."

As Taylor began to speak, he saw Schulz appear in the corner of the screen. He must have heard Taylor's voice and decided to investigate. He said something in German to his officer before taking over the comms himself.

"You have something important for me, Colonel?" he asked bluntly. "Please be short and to the point."

"Yes, Sir. The simple fact is, humans working for the Krys have infiltrated elements of government in Europe and elsewhere and are pouring petrol on the flames of war."

"And you have evidence of this?"

Taylor shook his head.

"Colonel, I have countless dead and wounded, and a war on our hands we could never have expected. Please do not give hope where there is none."

"You don't believe me?"

"How can I? Even if it is true, who are they? How can we find them, and how would it make any difference here? We're at war now, once more. Now please, I have much business to attend to."

And just like that, the conversation was over again. Ryan pointed to turn his attention to the news that had still been running but had been muted. It was a map of Europe showing some evolution of borders. Mitch put the sound back on to hear it was the drawing up of borders by the European Alliance. He could see it already included Spain, France, Italy, Portugal, Hungary, Slovakia, Serbia and Romania.

"They're heading for another World war."

"You have chosen the wrong side," stated Jafar.

"I wasn't aware we had chosen one," replied Taylor.

"You will not see harm come to the prisoners. So you are with the UEN."

"And should we not protect prisoners of war?"

"You assume they are all like me and Tsengal. They are not."

They turned their attentions back to the news as they caught sight of an alien soldier. Narration continued over the images.

"As the Spanish forces have pushed further into the Gafsa facility, we are getting reports that escaped prisoners are fighting alongside German soldiers. This video captured by one of the networks aerial drones appears to show exactly that, but representatives from the UEN have denied to comment on the matter."

Taylor looked more closely and could see the creature. It was wielding a Reitech weapon. He froze the image and zoomed in. In the background, he could just make out another of the Krys armed the same, and a human standing behind that.

"They've really done it," he whispered.

"How? How can they have gone from guarding the prisoners to fighting alongside them in such a short space of time?"

"It's not that big a leap," said Taylor. "These are people willing to fight to protect those prisoners, and once the camp was invaded, they'd take any help they could get. Think about it. Prison buildings being torn apart, and the detainees fighting for their lives, taking up arms beside the humans fighting for them is logical. On top of that, I bet the German UEN never expected it to go this far. I bet they haven't been able to muster troops quick enough to get there in support. That's why the air support went in so hard."

"Okay, well what do we do now?"

Taylor shrugged.

"We could go home. The US won't want a part in this if it can be avoided. We could go home and forget all about it," he stated cynically.

"After this, I can't believe you'd let this go."

"Those are our orders."

"Like that's bothered you. Let's say we stay, which side do we take?"

"I'd say that at least is pretty clear. Armand is UEN, UEN forces are enlisting Krys to fight with them. Enlisted armies of Krys, where do you think that is leading?"

"Agreed, so we're on the wrong side of the border."

"I'm not so sure. Local government here has been

opposed to any pro-alien standpoints. Looks to me like the borders are still being drawn up. God knows which side Belgium will end up on."

"Well, we need to know."

"Agreed. Monitor all local news networks, and try and get a feel for which side both public and government opinion is swaying. At present, we are an American vessel with no allegiance to either side, none that is implied anyway. The minute we pick a side, let's make sure we're in the right place, hey?"

"So we just wait?"

"For now, yes. We should be fine. We could all do with some rest. Double the number of guards on duty, and ensure you have enough crew ready to fly this boat at a moment's notice. If the need should arise to get the hell out of Dodge, I want it to be an option."

Taylor welcomed the rest, but long before the sun had risen, Ryan woke him. He groaned briefly until he remembered the seriousness of their situation.

"What is it?"

"Announcement from the Belgian President, regarding their membership to the UEN and their standpoint on the conflict."

"This is what we have been waiting for."

He rushed to the conference room, still wearing the clothes he had slept in. He sat down at the table and realised what was lacking. Every time he had been through such troubles, he had his close friends to hand, those from 2nd Inter-Allied. Now he was heading for another war and so few remained at his side.

The Belgian President was announced in Dutch, which meant nothing any of them. But as she stepped up to the podium, she began her address in English. The screen gave her name as President Mertens.

"Welcome to all of you. I have gathered you all here today, following emergency discussions on recent troubling matters. After considering all the evidence before us, and with our nation's best interests always at the centre of my concerns, I hereby announce our departure from the UEN and our condemnation of their failures, as well as recent recruitment of former enemy combatants. Following discussion with President Jacques, as of 0900 today, Belgium is a member of the European Alliance and will do everything in its powers to bring an end to alien inhabitation of Earth."

"So, we are on the right side of the border," said Ryan.

"I wouldn't be too hasty to say it," added Taylor.

"What? Are you not watching this?"

"I am. But Belgian is still a country strongly divided, on this as much as anything in their history. The Germans will know this and will be eager to replace the government with one in support of their needs. Of any nations bordering them, this is the easiest to draw to your cause with the right person at the reins."

"Sir, I'm getting reports of incoming aircraft from the German border, dozens of them," said a voice over the intercom.

"No, not this soon? They wouldn't invade, would they?"

"We got this announcement today, but I bet they've been discussing it since all this began. Somebody close to the President wants her out the way, and I bet you a task force has been waiting to move for some time."

"And the Belgian armed forces?"

"Won't be able to respond this fast, but we can."

"No way," replied Ryan.

"Why not? We've picked a side, but they don't trust us. We have an opportunity here to make a difference. We get the President to safety, and we could steal a victory out from under the UEN."

"Are those your orders?"

"They aren't orders. The crew must decide for themselves here. Gather all those who aren't on duty, and have those who are kept on an open channel to this room. It's time we set this to right."

Twenty-one gathered in the room moments after being called. Taylor knew they had no time to waste.

"There are a thousand things I could and should say to you all, give you some explanation. But time is not on our side. In short, the UEN are becoming an enemy who must be stopped, but the US doesn't seem interested. The Belgian President is soon to be in trouble, and she could be a valuable ally. I'm going to do everything I can to protect her, but you must decide for yourself. I know I have provided little explanation, but you know the UEN is allying with alien POWs, and you know the kind of man I am. So what'll it be?"

None of them responded, but they all looked to Ryan to do so for them.

"We're always with you, Colonel. Lead the way."

"Break out weapons and armour. Remember, we can't go stomping through the streets armed to the teeth. We'll drop in from the roof of the Parliament building and get her out and over the border into France."

"And what about the German forces en route?"

"We can only hope the Belgians scrambled a few fighters that slowed them down. If not, they'll already be there. Either way, we have to move fast. All agreed?"

"We're with you."

"Get us in the air!"

They were lifting off within twenty seconds, and the crew were rushing to gather equipment. He was quickly reminded that he was in command of a ship's crew, and not experienced marines as he was used to. Even worse, he was coming to realise it was all too easy.

When have I ever been able to see the whole picture like this?

The pieces seemed to be coming together too easily, but there was no more time to think on it.

The Deveron was soaring across the skies to the

government headquarters from where the President had made her speech. But as they drew nearer, they could make out other craft approaching from the north.

"Identify those craft," said Taylor.

He was on the bridge beside Ryan. Every one of the crew was now equipped in Reitech gear, but he knew few of them were experienced in using it.

"I need your three best marksmen."

"My five best are at the main door at the lower level. Take whichever you need."

"We'll be jumping onto the roof. You be ready to pick us up."

"That's the plan? And what about the Germans?"

"Keep 'em busy?"

"Keep 'em busy? Only way I got to keep them busy is let them blow holes in us."

'Relax; this is one of the finest vessels the US has ever built. You'll be fine."

"Well, that's a relief."

"Those are German ships," said an Ensign.

"They haven't fired on us. Don't provoke them," said Taylor.

He patted Ryan on the shoulder before pulling his helmet on and rushing out the door. Jafar was awaiting him and passed him his rifle. They hurried to the lower hull of the ship where the five men were waiting just as Ryan had said. They looked scared to death. Guarding the ship was the closest they'd ever come to combat. They were Navy seamen, not marines.

"Are you sure about this?"

"Sure, Jafar, why, you're not?"

"You always told me to look at things from all angles. You are making a lot of assumptions here."

"Facts are a luxury in this business. You know that."

He turned to the others. You three, Waters, Malok, and Hughes, you're coming with us. Stay close. He had to look at their nametags to remember their names; a fact he wasn't proud of.

"You jumped before?" he asked them.

They shook their heads.

"Set your boosters to auto, and they'll control our descent. When we hit the ground, you just follow me and Jafar, and keep an eye on our backs, you hear?"

They felt the reverse thrust kick in as the Deveron came in towards their location. Taylor hit the door switch, and it slid open, letting the fresh air pour in.

"This is it. Keep your eyes open and your weapon at the ready!"

He leapt from the edge the moment the ship came to a near halt in the sky. They were on the roof in a heartbeat, and there was not a sign of life.

"Get moving!" he shouted down the intercom to Ryan.

He looked around in surprise, and something didn't feel right at all. The sound of engines roared beside the building, and two ships lifted up into view before turning and soaring into the sky.

"Something's wrong."

"What?" asked Malok.

"A Presidential building with not a single guard in sight. No, something is wrong here."

"Colonel Taylor!" a voice called.

He turned to see Armand stepping out onto the roof from a nearby stairs.

No, can't be. He played us all along.

Now he knew why everything had fitted together so well in his head. It had been a carefully calculated plan to get him at his most vulnerable.

"You're a great fighter, Colonel, maybe even a great leader, but not the smartest!"

Troops poured out from the stairs behind him and from two other locations at their flank until over a hundred fully equipped soldiers encircled them.

"Oh, shit," he whispered, "When I shout, follow me, and do as I do."

"I can't say getting the President was important, but capturing you was an opportunity which I couldn't pass up, and you fell for it from day one," said Armand.

"Getting identified and recognised for who you are part of your plan as well?" he yelled back.

"Irrelevant now. Your only evidence is dead, and now I have you, too."

Taylor opened up his comms channel and left it open.

"So you are from Red 1?"

"Sure am, along with all the loyal soldiers you see around you. I thought we had an opportunity with you, Colonel. I thought you might be convinced to join the winning side, but clearly you'd rather die a martyr."

"You're gonna regret killing Tsengal because I'm not gonna kill you quick or easy."

"Big words for a man at the end of his days."

Engines roared overhead that gusted over the rooftop, kicking up dust around them all. The Deveron flew overhead and slowed to a crawling pace.

"Now!" Taylor shouted.

He hit his boosters and launched up into the air. The others followed suit and were hurled up into the sky up and over the ship. Taylor landed smoothly on the roof and Jafar beside him. He turned to see Waters rocketing towards him. He reached out and took hold of the sailor, grabbing him as he passed. Malok hit the deck hard but was okay. Hughes was coming in hard and fast. He hit the hull of the ship and slid along it. Taylor leapt after him and managed to get a hold on his leg but was pulled over the side. He thought he was going overboard but felt Jafar's iron grip around his ankle. As he was pulled, he called into his comms.

"Go!"

The engines roared. Gunfire zipped past the ship but

could do nothing against its armour. Taylor got to his feet in time to see Armand standing on the rooftop at an absolute loss.

"Sooner or later, I'm gonna kill you," Taylor said to himself.

A hatch slid open as they rolled in, and the turbulence began to get unbearable. He quickly got on his comms.

"Ryan, can you catch those two ships?"

"Bet your ass, Colonel."

"Do it!"

They felt the Deveron bank and go to full burn. Taylor brought up the ship's forward display screen on his Mappad. It only took them a few minutes to reach the two craft that were at a cruising speed and apparently in no rush. One was a small gunship and the other an armed transport.

"Ryan, knock the engines out on that gunship and bring us alongside the other."

"Sure about this, Sir?"

"No, but do it anyway."

The tracer coming on screen followed the crack of gunfire. The first volley narrowly clipped the aft of the gunship, and as they began to take evasive action, the second struck their engines. Their power was knocked out instantly, and they began to lose altitude. Taylor watched and waited to see if the crew would bail out. They did, and he gave a sigh of relief. He didn't want to see them dead.

"They are the enemy?" asked Jafar.

"Maybe, but they are also human. We kill only if we have to."

He looked to the other three who looked terrified.

"We have any explosives aboard?"

They shook their heads.

"Grenades?"

"No, Sir," replied Hughes, "We only carry what is necessary for the protection of the Deveron."

"Yeah, well, that's all fine and dandy when things go to plan. We'll just have to improvise."

"Ryan, we need to get aboard that ship, can you use the docking gear?"

"Airborne?" he asked.

"We need you to get that transport locked, even for just twenty seconds. Give us enough time to get aboard."

"I'll give it a shot."

The nose of the Deveron dipped as they came up under the transport that was half her size. They were at full burn now, but they couldn't outrun the Deveron.

"Just bear in mind, Sir, that we're in German airspace, not a place we want to be, considering."

"Got it, Ryan. We'll be quick."

Magnetic clamping arms extended from the Deveron as they came in close and took a hold on the hull. Taylor could see an access door now. He lifted his rifle and fired a dozen shots at the hinges.

"Do the honours," he said to Jafar.

The alien leapt onto the roof of the Deveron and got his grip inside the damaged door. With one big heave, he ripped it from the hull, and it flew off into the distance.

The two ships rocked as the transport shook violently.

"Sir, they're onto us. We can't keep them locked like this for long!" Ryan called over the comms.

"Let's move!"

He leapt out onto the roof and jumped up into the ship. Jafar and Hughes got inside with him, but as the other two were getting out onto the roof of the Deveron, the seal broke from the docking arms. The transport banked hard to get away from their ship. Malok was thrown overboard, but Waters managed to stay safe.

Hughes looked in horror as his crewmate descended rapidly.

"He'll be okay. The suit will get him down safe!"

"Safely into enemy territory, Sir!"

"We've got bigger things to worry about, right now! You stay here."

He readied his weapon and rushed up the ramp where he found Jafar already firing his weapon. The body of a soldier lay between him and them. It made him sick to see a human dead at their hands, but he knew it was unavoidable. He took up position beside Jafar and peered around the corner carefully. Three German soldiers lay in wait for them. One was using President Mertens as a human shield. The other two held rifles at the ready. All were equipped as they were.

"I am Colonel Mitch Taylor of the 2nd Inter-Allied Battalion, United States Marine Corps. Lay down your weapons!"

"You have no authority here!" one shouted back.

"Think about this. You're kidnapping a head of state!"

"We're at war, and we are under orders to detain President Mertens!"

"At war? Belgium declared independence from the UEN, a voluntary union!"

"And sided with those who are trying to kill us!"

"Do you want to die here?" he asked.

No response came.

"Because the only options here are we kill you, or you kill us and that ship out there blows you out of the sky. Handover the President and leave with your lives!"

"That's not happening!"

Taylor shook his head.

"Remember, you wanted this, not me!"

He pulled out a magazine from his webbing and threw it around the corner as if it were a grenade. He heard them shout in German and duck for cover. In that moment, he leapt out and fired two shots into one of their rifles. The rifle was smashed in two as the rounds penetrated his chest armour.

Jafar fired the next two shots doing exactly the same.

Only the man holding the President remained. He still held a pistol beside her, but now it was pointed at Taylor.

"Nobody else has to die here. We're taking the President whether we have to go through you or not. Hand her over and you can survive this."

"And if I give her to you, what stops you shooting us, anyway?"

"That's Colonel Taylor," said one of the men.

He could see they all knew his name even if they didn't recognise his face. For once his fame was working in his favour. He lowered his weapon and relaxed his body language, although he knew Jafar and Hughes had him covered.

"You must know this is wrong."

He could see in the man's eyes that he'd made up his mind.

"The President is coming with us or not at all. Those are our orders, and I am following them!"

His pistol turned towards the President. As the barrel touched her head, a shot zipped past Taylor from the barrel of Jafar's weapon, hitting the man just off centre between the eyes. Blood burst out from the exit wound and sprayed across the wall behind him. His body slumped, and the President remained frozen in fear.

Two more soldiers went for their pistols, but Taylor's rifle was up in a flash.

"No!" he shouted.

It was too late. The guns were in hand and being raised towards him. He fired at one, and Jafar took the other. They didn't stand a chance. But as one of them dropped, two shots rung out from his gun and hit the ceiling above. Sparks flew out and the lights cut out. Cries of panic came from down the corridor to the cockpit, and Taylor knew they were losing power and altitude.

"We gotta get out of here!"

He grabbed the President firmly and threw her rather unceremoniously onto his shoulder, hauling her back towards the hatch they had come from. The ship shook violently as the crew fought for control, but they were plummeting fast to the ground. Hughes was at the opening but frozen stiff. Taylor booted him out and leapt after him. He held on firm to Mertens as they fell. He could just about hear Hughes screaming and Waters alongside him.

Taylor looked around the sky for the Deveron, and then from out of a cloud it burst and soared towards them, plunging deep below where they were falling.

"Hit your boosters!"

The ship's nose lifted and came to hover a hundred metres below them. They fired the boosters and descended onto the hull. Taylor landed hard, and his knee buckled out as he hit the deck, but he put all his effort into maintaining his grip on the President. They fought the wind to get back to the opening and leapt inside. The hatch shut behind them, and he took a deep breath in relief.

"Get us the hell out of here, Captain!"

"Give me a direction, and we're gone, Sir."

"Paris!"

The engines roared once again as he took a moment to reflect on what had just happened.

"I underestimated Armand," he said.

"But we survived," replied Jafar.

"Just about."

He turned his attention to Mertens who was only partly recovered from the shock of all she had been through.

"Colonel, I thought you were for the other side."

"So did I, but let's just say I was wrong."

"Thank you. You've done me a great service, but I fear it will do little to keep my country free."

"One step at a time."

"You killed those men back there to save my life."

"And if I could have avoided it in any way, I would have."

"I know."

It brought a sombre tone to them all, Taylor above all else. Those were soldiers he could well have been fighting alongside in the wars. He told himself it was necessary. He'd killed the Krys without quibble, but this was entirely different. Killing humans left him feeling sick to the stomach.

He got up to his feet and helped the President up. "Come on, let's get to the bridge."

As he said it, an explosion rang out, and the Deveron rocked.

"We're hit," Ryan said over the comms.

Another explosion ignited, and they began to drop from the sky.

"We're going down! Get off the ship, Colonel!"

Taylor punched the door release, and it slid open above them. They all knew what they had to do. He grabbed hold of the President and jumped, with the others close behind. Seconds later, the ship crashed to the ground below them. They had exited at a hundred metres above the ground, in time to save them.

Debris and dirt erupted into the sky around them as they descended down on the crash site. The hull had buckled over a rocky riverbank edge, and Taylor could already see a gaping hole that had been torn in the starboard side.

It had all happened so fast, and none of them could believe their eyes. A few bodies of the crew were strewn across the grassland beside the wreckage where they had been thrown out through the damaged hull. Dust filled their lungs, and a sickly electrical burning smell filled the air. Taylor looked around. He didn't recognise where they were at all, but it was nowhere near civilisation. They all looked to him for answers, and all he could think was,

Oh, shit!

CHAPTER NINE

Taylor had no words to soften the blow they had just taken. He rushed in through the hole that had been punched in the side of the ship and had to step over two bodies as he headed for the bridge. He got to the entrance and found the door was bent and jammed half shut. He got a hold of it and tried to pull, but even with his suit did not have enough strength. He turned to see Jafar had joined him.

"Help me."

The two of them got a firm grasp and managed to force the door apart barely enough for him to squeeze through. All power was down, and the blast shields meant there was no light at all. He flicked on the torch on his helmet and peered around. Bodies were scattered across the bridge, and he looked from one to another to find survivors. A few groaned in pain but were unable to move. The he spotted Ryan sprawled out on the deck. He rushed to his side.

"What the hell hit us?"

"I was hoping you could have answered that question."

His voice was spluttered and weak, and it was clear he could not move his legs. It looked as if his spine had been severely damaged, but Taylor didn't want to say it.

"There's nothing you can do for us. Get going."

Taylor wanted to argue, but he knew the Captain was right.

"Good luck."

He got to his feet and rushed out through the smashed door. They got out from the ship to be accosted by Waters.

"Any survivors?"

"None that we can help right now."

"What happened to 'leave no man behind'?"

Taylor shook his head.

"A nice ideal to live by, but you know how many soldiers have been left behind in war? Ryan understands and wants us to go on, and that's exactly what we have to do. He lifted his Mappad device to get an understanding of where they were, but it could not find signal. His comms were out also.

"Impossible, someone must be jamming us. Where the hell are we?"

"Which side of the border are we?" asked Hughes.

"I'd say we're in the south of my country."

"You're sure of that?" asked Taylor.

"As sure as I can be, all things considered."

"Malok must be around here somewhere."

"Get real," replied Taylor. "He could be fifty clicks or more from our position, and with no way to communicate, he's on his own, same as we are."

"You came after me, why?" asked the President.

"Sides are being drawn up. I chose mine, as you chose yours."

"Well, thank you, for trying at least."

"Oh, we aren't done yet. We have to get into France. As the legitimate leader of your country, you can be reinstated with a little help. If you die, it's all for nothing."

This is just going from shit to worse, he thought.

He was starting to realise it had all gone downhill since the moment he met Armand. The gladiatorial combat and puppet strings he had been pulled along by were bad, but nothing compared to what shit Armand had landed him in.

He looked at his watch. It was a long time till sundown. He flipped open the top to reveal a compass, his only means of navigation now. He looked around. The countryside around them was predominantly thick woodland.

"We'll have good visual cover, but that's not gonna save us from thermal imaging."

"Then we should move quickly."

"Southwest it is. Let's move."

"So we just keep walking and hope to reach France?"

"We'll reach it all right, Hughes. This ain't such a big country, no offence."

"Why don't we look for help nearby? We have their President for God's sakes. Surely the locals will help?"

Taylor shook his head.

"US forces and an alien roaming the lands with the nation's President. Anyone we go to is just as likely to think we're the kidnappers and immediately report us to the authorities. We can't trust anyone this side of the border. It can't be more than fifty clicks to it."

"Fifty clicks?" Waters shouted.

Taylor grabbed the man by the frontal plate of his armour.

"You get your shit together. Fifty clicks is a walk in the park, considering the alternative. With any luck, it's closer. I want to be there before the sun rises tomorrow."

"We have no food, only the water in our suits," said Hughes.

"You Navy boys have had it too easy for too long. Water is all we need. Let's get moving."

Jafar led the way. Taylor knew he would terrify anyone they came across, but he was thankful to have someone dependable at the front. The two seamen with them still looked terrified, but he didn't blame them. They'd just lost their ship and most of the crew with it. As they reached the edge of a thick forest, Taylor turned to look back at the Deveron one last time. The stricken ship had done him and many others years of loyal service.

"Good luck, Ryan," he whispered as he turned and carried on.

"You'd leave those crew to get me out?" asked Mertens.

"Nothing more I can do for them. Had I the support I had in the war, I'd call in for assistance and get them out, but we did this of our own accord. My commanding officer will want my head for this."

"Coming after me, or losing that ship?"

"Both."

"You really are that officer we have seen so much on TV recently, aren't you? The Gladiator some have called you."

He didn't answer, as he wasn't proud of the fact.

"So it is you. You're the last person I would have expected to come to my aid. Do you regret it yet?"

"No room in a marine's mind for regret. We keep moving forward, improvise, and overcome."

"But you're not a marine today, are you? Not here on their orders or interests."

He was silent.

"So you've decided to join the Alliance? Even though America wants nothing to do with this conflict?"

She kept pushing until finally he knew he had to respond.

"I didn't fight over these lands for nothing. Way I see it, this is as much my home as the States is now, and I won't stand by and watch half the World rip itself to pieces."

"Even if that means fighting a human against human war?"

"I can't see how that can be avoided, can you?"

"One of the key reasons I did what I did is because we have irrefutable evidence that the UEN is freeing alien prisoners and recruiting them into their armies, and that they were being prepared for it months ago."

"You can't be serious?"

"I am. As a key representative of the UEN, I have been at the forefront of discussions. The UEN has been moving to find ways to integrate alien POWs into the World populace and find a way they can contribute to society. Maybe they weren't training them to use weapons, but the foundations were there before all this began."

Taylor shook his head.

"That figures."

She seemed surprised.

"How so?"

"I just heard from a reliable source that humans working for the Krys, or what look to be human at least, have infiltrated various levels of government on Earth."

"And you have proof of this?"

"No," he sighed, "and nobody I have so far contacted is willing to entertain the idea."

"But you know this for certain?"

He nodded.

"Yes, that would explain how all this escalated so quickly. But how can we tell who is working with them or not?"

"No idea. I know of only one who is definitely with them, Councillor Armand."

"Ah, yes, that little worm."

They'd got half a kilometre and in the middle of an opening when a missile smashed into the ground beside them, showering them with dirt. A moment later they heard a copter buzz by.

"Run!" he shouted.

He didn't know what they were running towards, but he couldn't think of anything else to do. The copter was far out of reach of their weapons.

"One copter? Why one?"

"They must be worried about attracting too much attention, Hughes. We must be closer to the border than we thought!"

They reached an embankment and before them was a road and sign reading 'Welcome to Saint-Hubert'. The sign was brand new.

"Saint-Hubert, this place was devastated in the war. It's still only a small community," said Mertens.

"It'll do!" he replied as they kept running.

"How can they help us?"

"That copter won't keep firing once we're in the cover of enough civilians."

"You'd risk that?"

"If it means not dying, yeah!"

The copter was coming back for another pass when they hit a stroke of luck, a school bus with fifteen children aboard. Taylor rushed out in front of the vehicle that brought the driver to a quick halt. He didn't like doing it, but he knew it was the only thing that would save their lives.

"Get up beside the bus!"

He looked up to see the copter pass without firing, and he could see the German markings clearly now. He'd prayed they wouldn't open fire, with the potential for collateral damage, but it was as much a gamble as anything else. He rushed to the door of the bus and ripped it open. It tore from the hinges, and he threw it aside into the grass.

"Inside now!"

The children aboard screamed in fear as they stepped inside, but it reached its peak at Jafar climbing in.

"Everyone be quiet!" shouted Taylor.

It did nothing, but he repeated the order and expected it to be followed. Mertens got to her feet and spoke to them, but Taylor didn't understand a word of it. She finally turned to him.

"Okay?" he asked her.

She nodded in response.

Taylor put his rifle over the driver's arm. The women looked in an utter panic.

"Keep moving into the town."

"Please, Sir, we don't want any trouble."

Taylor put his hand around her head and turned it, despite her trying to resist.

"You see who that is? That is your President. We're trying to save her life. Do you want to help, or do you want to be responsible for her death?"

The driver was terrified, but her expression turned to confusion on recognising the President.

"Drive!"

How did it come to this? Hijacking a school bus and on the run from UEN forces? Has the whole World gone mad?

"Where are you taking us?" pleaded the woman.

She was shaking and crying, and that made Taylor feel even crappier than he already did. Mertens stepped up beside her.

"It'll be fine, but I need you to do this, okay?"

It was the first time he had heard her speak to her compatriots in English, and he knew it was as much for his benefit as for theirs. She turned back to him.

"We can't keep this up. I will not endanger these children, not for anything."

"But you would risk our lives? The lives of US personnel who don't owe you anything? Who have no reason to be here, besides what they think is the right thing to do. Look at us. We owe you nothing, and we have lost many friends today. That was to protect you."

"I am very thankful for your efforts, Colonel, but don't expect me to believe you did this out of pure selflessness. You chose the wrong side, and you are looking for a way to redeem yourself, so I tick more boxes than simply making you feel good about yourself."

Great, another politician with no care in the World for those who serve to protect her!

He knew he shouldn't be surprised. Although her argument made some sense, he didn't like hearing it.

"You were a hero to this world, Colonel, and rightly so. But in these past years you have been a shadow of your former self. You have let yourself be paraded around for the entertainment of the lowest common filth in society, but you can be the man you used to be. Be the soldier you used to be."

"I don't need any lectures from a politician," he snapped back, "Where were you when the World needed you?"

Yet again she made some sense, but he'd never admit it to her.

"Do the right thing, Colonel. If we don't protect the next generation, what was it all ever for?"

"Right, stop the bus!"

The driver slammed the brakes on and froze where she sat. Taylor knelt in close to talk with her.

"Get the kids off the bus and take them back to town. Don't cover for us. Don't lie to anyone. We don't need your protection. We just need the vehicle. Got it?"

She nodded her head in agreement.

"Do it."

She carefully and slowly got to her feet as if she was suspicious he was actually going to let her leave. He hated having made her feel that way, but there was no time to apologise over it.

"What are you doing?" asked Mertens.

"Okay, we won't put these kids in any more danger, but we need this bus."

He pulled open the door and let the driver do the rest before turning back to the few companions he had.

"Hughes, think you can drive this thing?"

"It looks older than my Pop's, but yeah."

"Get on it and get us moving."

He looked around, the sailor was right. It was a rickety old transport that looked as if it had been brought out of military service.

"Come on, Hughes, minute they realise we have ditched the kids, we are fair game."

"Then why did we ditch 'em?"

"God knows," he said, sighing.

Hughes leapt into the driver's seat and got them moving quickly.

"I can drive this, but I got no idea where we're going."

Taylor looked over to the navigation, but like his Mappad, it wasn't working.

"Take the road to Gedinne. We can cross the border

near there," Mertens said.

"You sure about that?"

"That I know my own country? Yes, I'm sure, Colonel."

"Do as the President says."

They could see the signs in front of them and did as she said. Taylor took a seat, relieved that they finally seemed to be on the home run. He sat next to the driver and facing backwards to the rest of the seating. Mertens was sitting nearest him and seemed surprisingly calm with all they had been through.

"What else do you know about all this?" he asked her.

"I'm afraid to say everything else is public information. The last communication I had with anyone was your President. I pleaded with him for the United States to intervene at the prison camps to aid in a peaceful solution."

"And?"

"And it failed…"

Taylor looked out of the window for some sight of the craft that had stalked them, but it was gone.

"Think they've had enough?"

"Not likely, Waters, but we can hope."

Twenty minutes later Hughes let out a cry of excitement, and Taylor turned to see it was a sign pointing to the border crossing.

"Just two kilometres out!"

"What will you do once we get to France?" the President asked Taylor.

"Push my contacts in the UK and see where I can get to. If I can't get support back home, that's my next safe bet. I have friends there."

"And do what then?"

He shook his head.

"I don't know. The World's going to shi… to hell. And this time it isn't as simple as fighting those in front of me."

"Welcome to my world."

He opened his mouth to speak but was silenced by a scream from Hughes.

"Shit!"

Taylor turned to see a line of gunmen blocking the road. They wore Reitech equipment but no insignia over plain black uniforms. He reached over and grabbed the wheel, tugging it to one side. The bus veered violently off to one side, ramming a car beside it as the line of gunmen opened fire.

"Get down!" he ordered.

He heard Hughes yelp as a shot went into his arm. Bullets ripped through the outer skin of the bus with little resistance at all. Taylor couldn't see anything from where he was and had to hope for the best now. A moment later they heard glass shatter, and the bus rocked as they burst through a huge pane and then smashed into a wall.

The impact sent them all tumbling from their positions. Taylor hit the main console at the front of the bus, smashing into the inside of the windscreen, and then back down to the seat. He got to his feet, doing his utmost to ignore the pain and get a handle on the situation.

"Get up!"

He looked out of the windows. They were inside a modern shopping mall. He drew out his pistol and offered it to Mertens.

"Know how to use this?"

Mertens was in her mid-fifties. She was more than a little overweight and hardly looked like the gun toting type, but he had to do something.

"Can you use it or not?" he insisted.

"I can learn quickly if I need to," she responded, snatching it from his grasp.

Fighting spirit, it's a start.

"Everyone off the bus!"

The door was jammed shut, but it was fortunately weak. He kicked it and it flew from its hinges. Screams of panic rang out from around them, as people went from concern for the occupants to fleeing from men with guns. He quickly surveyed the scene and led them further into the facility. He looked back. Hughes was nursing his wounded arm and wasn't even holding his rifle that was now slung on his back. Jafar was holding up the rear.

They took a bend, and the only way was up via automated stairs. As they rode up to the next floor, Taylor looked at the faces of Hughes and Waters. They both looked ready to give up.

"Hughes, get that weapon in hand. You haven't got time to bleed! Mertens, you stick at my back, no matter what."

Jafar was the last one off the stairs, and as he did so, gunfire raced past his head. Taylor jumped to his aid. A metre high wall ran alongside the top of the stairs, providing a perfect firing position to shoot down on those chasing them. He popped up from cover, quickly took aim, and fired three shots. Two hit the man's armour, and the third struck his hand, almost taking it off at the wrist.

He ducked back down as he head the screams of the fallen soldier. Jafar fired the next shots, but he could not see the result of them.

"Who are these people?" asked Waters.

"Soldiers loyal to Armand. That's all you need to know."

"What are we gonna do?"

"Shoot back!"

He got up and fired again. It was enough to drive their attackers back, but he knew they'd already be working on ways to flank their position. Mertens tried to get up to fire, but Taylor hauled her back down.

"I gave you that gun as a last resort. You do not stick your head out while we're still in this fight."

She was at first offended by the way he spoke to her, but then thankful. He took a few more shots before getting to his feet and dragging her with him.

"Come on, let's keep moving!"

They were on the first floor of the mall now, and the

floor divided and split with an open drop down to the ground floor below.

Up or down? Up or down?

It wasn't easy to decide when so few options presented themself.

"Where are we going?" screamed Waters.

"You don't know, do you?" asked Hughes. "This is fucked. It's so fucked."

Taylor turned and slapped the man hard in the face.

"Man the fuck up. We've got a job to do, and we're gonna get it done."

Screams rang out from below, and he looked down to the ground level. Troops were pouring through the crowd looking for them.

"Follow me."

He headed for the next escalator, but this time he sprinted up it. They took up position as they had done before.

"How many floors in this place?" Taylor asked Mertens.

She shrugged. "I'm sorry, but I've never been here before."

He looked around for some more information and found the board with a map of the site.

Why didn't I think to look?

He hadn't visited a mall in more years than he could remember. It showed another two floors above them.

"What do you think, go for the roof?" he asked Jafar.

"You're the boss."

"That's a big help."

"Here they come," said Waters.

Taylor lifted his rifle over the ledge and took aim.

"Just a few shots to keep their heads down and then we move."

He fired first. One brushed off one of the soldiers' helmets. One missed all together, and another clipped a man's ear and got him screaming as it took the tip off.

"Go!"

They rushed up to the next level but did not stop until they hit the roof. As they burst out of the door, Mertens curled over gasping for air. She wasn't able to handle the exertion being placed on her, and he could see the Navy boys suffering also.

"What now?" Jafar asked.

"You too? How about somebody else comes up with the answers for once?"

He went over to the western edge of the roof and looked out towards the border.

"We could jump it?"

"I don't think we have the power left to do it."

"I don't think we have a choice," he replied, "We jump as far as we can, and carry on from there on foot. It's our best hope."

He knew the others had heard him, and he looked to them for an opinion. None responded.

"We keep pushing, or it's over, and it was all for nothing. Did we fight all this time to give up now? Did the Deveron go down for nothing? Was the sacrifice of her crew, our friends, for nothing?"

Footsteps thundered up the stairs behind them, and they knew they had less than a minute to make a decision.

"We're gonna make this, you know why? Because we deserve to; too much shit has happened today for us to fail now. So what the hell? Let's do this!"

He grabbed Mertens and threw her over his shoulder and ran along the rooftop. The others were quick to follow, not because they believed they could make it, but being left behind was a more frightening concept.

The boosters launched them from the rooftop. They covered a few hundred metres when Taylor's boosters began to give out, and the last of his power was automatically diverted to bring him to a quick and safe descent. He landed in the middle of the road to the border, causing cars to veer off it to avoid them.

The others landed around him soon after, but they knew they were a long way short of France. It was within reach and yet so far away. A driver of a car that had slid to a halt before them ran from his car. Taylor moved up and quickly took it as cover.

"What now?" Hughes asked.

"I'm not gonna be shot in the back. We turn and fight these bastards."

"With what? We're outnumbered, and you can't have much more ammunition left than me."

"And that is a reason to quit, a reason to give up? Thinking like that would have seen an end to humanity! Load up and prepare to fight!"

He slammed in a new magazine and put his muzzle down on the roof of the car. Troops were amassing. He'd counted a few dozen figures already taking up position.

How did it come to this? A hundred battles, and it could all end with so few at my side on some crappy stretch of road?

It was hard to see a way out for any of them. He turned to Jafar for answers, but he had none.

"A thousand things we could have done differently and not ended up here, Jafar."

"And a thousand things you could have done which would have killed you sooner."

Taylor smiled, patting his friend on the shoulder.

"Sure beats rotting in a cell."

He grabbed Mertens and shoved her down behind the car.

"You don't have to die here," he said.

She seemed baffled.

"This car here. Get in, and we'll move to the next one. Once we're in cover, you can pull away. They can't know you're still with us. You can make it to the border, you can…"

"No," she stated firmly.

"I've seen you are important to humanity as any president, Colonel. Presidents come and go every few years, but you are constant."

"Maybe not for much longer," he jested. "You know this story ain't gonna have a happy ending, right?"

She nodded.

Stubborn! I like this President.

There were no sirens in the distance. No police rushing to the scene or help coming for them. Taylor had never felt so abandoned since he had been in a prison cell. The black clothed gunmen approached their position, using the cover of the vehicles that were stacked up. Finally, as they finally took up positions, one of them called out to him with an amplifier of some kind.

"Colonel Taylor! Our fight is not with you! President Mertens is under arrest for breach of the public trust and illegal use of her powers. Hand her over, and this can end peacefully. She is not your responsibility. She is not your problem. Give her up so that she can face sentencing in a European court, and you may walk free."

"You mean UEN court?" he asked.

"That is Europe, and anybody who says different is a troublemaking rebel intent on dividing our people."

"Christ, who is this guy?" asked Mertens.

"Someone who is really starting to piss me off," replied Taylor.

Taylor took aim at the man through his sights. He

squeezed the trigger without hesitation. The bullet hit his throat and instantly silenced him. Blood spurt out from the wound. Gunfire returned almost simultaneously, forcing them to duck down as the car they were sheltering behind was peppered with fire.

"Not much of a diplomat, are you, Colonel?" shouted Mertens.

The shooters started encircling their position, and Taylor saw one appear at their flank. He opened up with his rifle, and the man ducked back down. Jafar was doing the same at the other end of the car while Waters and Hughes kept it up at the centre. Taylor knew it was his last magazine, but he'd accepted the end, just as he had done so many times before.

His rifle was out. He reached over and grabbed his pistol from Mertens and kept firing. The gunmen were surrounding their position, and he knew he didn't have long before they were completely exposed to the troops working their way around the flanks.

All hope seemed lost, but just as the thought passed through Taylor's mind, engines roared towards them, kicking up dust. He looked up to see copters fly into view and come to a hover over them. One was Rains' distinctly painted monstrosity, with a distressed stars and stripes and a reaper carrying a scythe.

It must be a dream.

"Impossible!" he yelled.

Troops leapt from the copters and landed all around. The first face he saw was Parker's. She was wearing the full gear of an Inter-Allied NCO. He couldn't believe his eyes, no matter how much he wanted it to be true. She rushed towards him and pushed him down into the cover of the car.

"Are you okay? Are you okay?"

He could barely find the words to respond. He got up and could see dozens of allied troops flooding through the streets, pursuing the gunmen who had plagued them since the crash of the Deveron.

"How are you here?"

Another man approached, another who was unmistakeable. Sergeant Silva, his arm replaced with a bionic. He looked as purposeful as ever.

"It was his idea," Eli said, pointing to the Sergeant Major.

"Hit me," he said.

She looked at him funny.

"Hit me, or I won't believe it's real."

He expected a slap, but Parker punched him in the face. His head rocked back before recovering with a smile as blood trickled from his nose.

"Eli, meet President Mertens."

"Ma'am," she said with a small bow.

"How are you here? America wanted nothing to do with this?"

"We aren't here as Americans, Ma'am. We're here for him, and that means we're here for you."

Taylor turned around once again. The black clothed gunmen were in full retreat. Rains' copter put down in an opening between the vehicles and rushed out in person to greet Taylor.

"Son of a bitch, you're still alive? Means we didn't fly out here for nothing!"

"Ma'am, if you'll join us," said Parker. "We've fooled this band of gunmen, but this isn't the US getting involved. This really is all we have. We need to get back into friendly territory."

"Lead the way!"

Taylor ran alongside the two of them.

"I thought you were done with the Corps?" he asked.

"Not by choice. I left for you, but while I can have both, I'll take everything I can get! Now let's get the hell out of here, before you attract anymore trouble!"

He could barely believe it were true. After all the hardship they had faced the past few days, they had been saved. He rushed to Rains' copter as quickly as he could. Even as they were lifting off, they could see more gunmen and vehicles rolling up to the scene.

"Close call," he whispered.

"Should be your middle name!" Eli said, smiling.

A minute later and they were in French air space. Three fighters raced up to their flanks.

"What now?"

"It's okay, Mitch. They're here to escort us to Paris."

"How'd you wrangle that?"

"We told the French they could either escort us in or shoot us down."

"That's a relief," he replied sarcastically.

CHAPTER TEN

"I thought we were going for Paris?

Taylor looked at the military base where they were coming in to land.

"Sorry to disappoint you, Colonel," replied Rains. "This is Meaux, a base set up last year, and very shiny it is, too!"

Taylor was first out the door and down the ramp once they were on the ground, and General Dupont was awaiting them with a few dozen soldiers.

"Good work, Colonel!"

They were the last words he ever expected to hear from the Frenchman who had become so embittered towards him, but that was all he was going to get. The General stepped past and offered his hand to Mertens.

"Welcome to France. Please come this way."

He turned back for a moment.

"Colonel, Commander Phillips is en route for liaison

purposes. I'll meet with both of you in thirty minutes in my office."

As eager as Taylor was to rest, he knew there was work to be done and was glad to finally have managed to get an audience with someone who had the power to do something. He looked around to see those who had come to his rescue. There were no officers among them, except for the pilots. He counted a little over thirty marines. Silva and Parker seemed to be in charge. He paced up to the RSM who looked mighty pleased with himself.

"How on Earth did you manage this?"

"Heard you were in trouble, and it didn't take much to convince the Lieutenant," he stated, pointing over to Rains who was slumped against the landing gear of his copter. The pilot gave off a mock salute.

"You're crazy, whole lot of you. No way White signed off on this."

"Nope," replied Silva.

"So you're AWOL, and entered a sovereign nation's air space to raise hell." He paused for a minute, "And I can't thank you enough, you crazy fools. Couldn't have done it without you."

"I wish we could have got more of the unit here, but this is just about all we could get away without raising flags. As far as the Corps is concerned, we're in Arizona on exercise."

"And due back when?"

"Tomorrow," replied Silva.

"And you?" he asked Parker.

"I quit the job, and I'm back. Not officially, but I'm here."

He looked out to the rest of them who were waiting for some news or explanation.

"I know you must all be eager to know what the hell's going on! All I can tell you at this stage is that a war is brewing on Earth, the likes of which even we have not seen, a war amongst humankind. I can't give you much more at this time. The only thing you should know, the Krys are in on it, and will use it to exploit a weakness."

It didn't seem like news to them, so he continued.

"As far as I know, the United States wants no part of this growing conflict, but I cannot and will not accept that! I didn't fight all these years, only to see the World go to shit while we sit back and enjoy some kind of peace that can never last. This new alliance, a European Alliance, may be our best hope of getting through this. I'm committing myself to their service, but I cannot ask you to do the same. I am in all your debt for what you did for me here, but now you must make a choice for yourselves. You can go home, or you can come with me."

There was no answer.

"You know we got the shit jobs in the war. The jobs no other sons of bitches believed could be done. I fully intend to take up that mantle once more, but I will think no lesser of any marine who would return home and see an end to this. If that is your desire, step forward now, or stay the distance."

Nobody moved an inch.

"We're with you, Colonel, just as we always have been," Silva boomed.

"Then ready yourselves because the work is just about to begin. I meet with General Dupont and Commander Phillips shortly, and I fully intend to offer our services to whatever end may be necessary."

The all nodded in agreement as they sat about in the sun, as calmly as if they were at home. Nothing seemed to shake them anymore. Those who stood before him were some of the most experienced veterans the World had seen in a few hundred years, and they knew it. He nodded in acceptance and turned to go to Dupont.

Taylor strolled alone through the base of Meaux. It was an impressive sight. Row upon row of brand new buildings and dozens of armoured vehicles and jeeps which looked like they'd never seen war, though he knew they had. He walked past an engineers' workshop where dozens of soldiers were working to overhaul war-damaged trucks. They were parked up bumper to bumper in a parking lot to one side of the huge hangar.

Bullet holes riddled some of their paintwork, but others were far worse with twisted chassis and bodies almost ripped in half. As he carried on past the structure, he found another line up of the same vehicles fully rebuilt and ready to use.

Just in time to go back to hell.

He got some odd looks as he headed for the General's office on foot.

His American flag was in plain view for all to see, and he still carried his rifle slung over his back. No one else he passed carried weapons nor wore armour, as per regulation, but nobody stopped to question him. He finally reached the HQ building. As he approached, the two MPs at the entrance looked desperate to pounce on him.

"Hand over your weapons," one said.

He passed his rifle over and was thankful to have it off his shoulder, but as they looked down to his pistol, he shook his head.

"You're not having my sidearm."

"You may not enter armed."

"Not in peacetime, but don't you know there's a war on? I've had too long a day to put up with this."

"Let him through!" yelled a voice.

He looked up. Dupont's head was poking out of a window and bellowing the command that could not be refused. They reluctantly let him pass. He took pleasure in their discomfort.

"Thank you, Gentlemen," he added, just to rub salt into the wound.

He stepped through into Dupont's office and found

the General shaking his head.

"You really do have a problem with authority, Colonel."

"Yes, Sir," he replied, smiling.

"But as much as I dislike your manner, I will happily admit you are a great soldier."

"Marine..."

"Whatever."

The door opened, and Phillips stepped through. He hadn't seen the Commander in years and quickly outstretched his hand in friendship.

"Come to join the fight, Sir?"

"Good to see you're still alive, Mitch, but I'm here purely as a correspondent. I can have no part in any potential conflict, not while the United Kingdom remains neutral."

"Neutral? What, are you kidding me?"

"Sorry, Colonel, but that's not my decision. Our government has declared neutral status and has condemned the activities of the UEN. Our Prime Minister has not gone as far as departing from the UEN, but he might as well have."

"Politics aren't my thing, Sir. I'm a fighting man."

"We both know that's bollocks. You repeatedly stick your nose in where it isn't wanted and stir up trouble."

Taylor shrugged. He couldn't disagree.

"Gentlemen, may we get on to business," said Dupont.

He walked around his desk and took a seat, gesturing for them to join him.

"I've got you here for a closed meeting because both of you are from nations who have so far had no involvement with the recent conflict, and therefore I cannot allow you into briefings or any other such matters. Everything that happens here is strictly between us. I am doing this because I think both of you can make a difference here, and we need allies."

"I'm a long way off the reservation, General, so spit it out."

"This discussion is off the record, and I will deny any involvement with it, or that you were ever even here, should you spill anything that is said. At 1800 hours today, the European Alliance will declare war on the UEN unless certain demands are met."

Taylor knew it was coming but not so soon. The statement took him aback.

"I think it's pretty clear what those demands will be, and that the UEN will not accept them. Gentlemen, be under no illusions, before the day is through, we will be at war."

"Surely this can be avoided?" pleaded Phillips.

"I wish to God it could be, but forces beyond my understanding appear to be forcing us in this direction, one which now cannot be avoided. Colonel, you tried to tell me you believed the Krys had placed human agents among us, do you still believe that to be the case?"

"Yes, Sir, I know it to be true."

"A relief in one regard, that it was an external force which led us to this and not our own humanity, but also a terrifying fact. I did not believe you because it sounded crazy. It still sounds crazy. Do you have any proof whatsoever that this is the case? And if so, how do we tell who is working for alien interests and who is not?"

"I wish I had those answers for you, General, but I don't, but I know a man who does."

"Then get him here immediately. Who is this man?"

"Councillor Armand."

The General was silenced.

"Can't be!"

"He had one of my marines killed, the only one who knew about these Krys agents, the only evidence I had. He tried to kill me soon after."

"Councillor Armand? He has a lot of sway in the UEN. You're telling me he is the one behind all this? The one who has brought us to a state of war?"

"Just one of the many players, I believe."

"Come on, Gentlemen, this is absurd," stated Phillips.

"As absurd as an alien invasion on Earth?" asked Taylor. "I wish it were not true. But Tsengal saw this with his own eyes. He identified Armand as an enemy agent, and saw maybe millions more humans on Red 1 who are just like Armand. His last order from Colonel Chandra was to return to me with this info that she knew could end us all. She died getting the information to us, and so did Tsengal and many others. I know it to be true."

Dupont scratched his head as he tried to make sense of the situation.

"Even if this is true, and I am almost at a point at which I believe it, how can we prove it? If they have agents among us, we need to know how to find them."

"The only person in the World I know for certain is one of them is Councillor Armand. I propose a mission to retrieve him."

"Careful, Colonel, you are stepping dangerously close to an act of war. Your country isn't even in this, and neither is mine. We shouldn't even be part of this kind of talk."

"You can leave anytime you like," Dupont replied.

They both looked to the Commander and hoped for his support, but he was deeply conflicted.

"We didn't fight all these years just to be beaten now, did we?" Taylor asked. "If we lay down now and let these agents succeed, we might as well have not bothered at all and let our World fall."

"Then let's take this information to our superiors..."

"What information? At the moment, all there is to go on is what I know to be true. The only other man who witnessed Tsengal's revelations is now gone. The video records destroyed. Who will take my word, one marine? Who would take that word and make world -changing decisions based upon them? I don't know if you looked around recently, but I'm not exactly popular. I don't even have the trust of the Alliance yet."

"Maybe not. Getting President Mertens out has gone a long way, though."

Great, they risked their lives, and we lost friends to earn a pass to getting that trust?

"Commander, I need Inter-Allied back together. I need you to get me those troops. As a force we are unstoppable."

"That's what worries me. You'll raise all kinds of hell. But this isn't the war, Colonel. Human lands are not overrun with Mechs," Phillips replied.

"No, it isn't, but be under no illusions, we are at war. Whether you like it or not, your country is going to be drawn into this war. Better we get a head start than fight an uphill battle, don't you think?"

"I am sorry, Colonel. I might agree with some of your ideas, but I cannot interfere in a conflict we have no part in."

He got up and moved to the door but turned back last minute.

"I cannot support your actions. I cannot order the reinstatement of the British elements of 2nd Inter-Allied."

Taylor dipped his head and sighed.

"However, I will inform Captain Grey that you have been asking after him. He has a training exercise coming up. I'll be sure to see he is prepared for all eventualities and made aware of your intentions."

Taylor looked up and smiled.

"Thank you."

"I cannot order him to help you nor deploy to you, but I will cover for him if he chooses to come to your aid."

He nodded in appreciation, as he knew that was a long step over the line for the Commander.

"Good day, Gentlemen, and good luck. You'll need it."

With that, he left the room. Taylor looked back to Dupont and couldn't believe for a moment that they were now in a room working with one another. Two men who had grown to detest the sight of one another, and yet now worked as one."

"Colonel, I won't lie to you. I cannot take this information I have to the Alliance without some solid proof. Neither can I authorise you to enter UEN territory on any grounds. War will be declared in less than five hours. When that happens, you will stand little chance of getting your hands on the Councillor. If he truly is a Krys agent, it could change everything."

"What would you have me do?"

"I will not command you to do anything. I cannot, and neither can I authorise any mission within UEN territory while we are at peace. However, if an American officer were to do so of his own volition, whether you succeed or fail, there would be no repercussions, except against yourself, of course."

"America may not be in this war yet, but we will be, and when we do join, I want a fighting chance."

"Colonel, your marines may use the facilities of this base; food, ammunition, and anything else you need, beyond that you are on your own. When and if you step over the border into UEN territory, you will remain on your own. We cannot provide assistance, and we cannot come for you should you or any of your troops be captured."

"What are they gonna do, put us in a cell? In the wars, we fought behind enemy lines where to be captured meant certain death. This'll be a walk in the park compared to that."

"Then I pray you can bring Armand back to us. Once war is declared, he will be considered an enemy of the state, and we can pursue interrogation to the full extent of our law."

"I'll bring the bastard back here, or die trying. I'll need a ship; something civilian that isn't going to attract attention. Something with British identity would be ideal."

"You'll have it."

"I need it now."

"One hour, and I'll have something for you."

He nodded in appreciation.

"You know I was wrong about you, Colonel. Your insubordination and lack of respect for authority led me to detest you, but now I understand it. You are a man born to fight, born to win wars. You are in your element at this very point, and there is not a man I would trust more to take on such a task."

"Thank you, General, and you're still a son of a bitch, but at least you're on the right side."

He left the room. As he walked out of the building, he snatched his rifle from the MP who was waiting with it. Taylor's private comms was ringing in his ear. He lifted his Mappad and answered the call. He realised it was coming in from HQ, but his finger had already touched the button to accept the call. General White's face was projected before him, and he continued walking back to his comrades. White looked confused and angry at the same time.

"Taylor? The Deveron emergency beacon has been activated from a location within Belgium, and I'm getting some intel that she was shot down. The ship is unreachable. Last time we spoke, you were aboard the ship and in Brussels. Explain to me what the hell is going on out there."

"It's a little difficult to explain, Sir."

"Difficult? Looks like half the World is going to shit, and you're out there acting like a cowboy, and getting caught up in just about everything you could be. It wouldn't be such a leap to make to assume you were at the centre and cause of all this!"

"I think that's a bit of a bit assumption to make, General."

"Well, it's all I can do when I can barely reach you, and you're a fucking hurricane of shit!"

It wasn't a pleasant comment, and he didn't know how to respond.

"Where are you now?"

"Sorry, Sir, but I can't say."

"Can't say? Who the hell do you think..."

"Sir, you'll just have to trust me on this one."

"Enough of this bullshit, Taylor. You're finished. I don't give a goddamn where you are, but you're gonna find the first civilian transport you can and get yourself Stateside before the day is through. You will report directly to me, so we can get some idea of what the hell's going on. You've really screwed the pooch on this one, Mitch. Don't expect to be holding onto your command when you get back."

"What command, Sir? I lost that a long time ago when you made me the poster boy for the Corps and had me shuffled around the country pandering to crowds and killing for sport."

White seemed taken aback by his retort and stunned for a moment.

"You just get your ass back here."

"Negative, Sir. I've got a job to do and a responsibility to all those I fought for during the war."

"Don't screw your career any further, Mitch. You're already walking a fine line here."

"Career? Look at the news, Sir. We're way past this. Trouble is on our doorstep, and you're pissing about over some insubordination charges? I'm gonna do exactly what

I have to do and need to do, and no less."

"What the hell are you talking about?"

"The World is in far greater danger than you realise, General. I have an opportunity which could make a difference, that could save us from something terrible, and I'm gonna take it."

White opened his mouth to speak, but Taylor simply cut the transmission off. He knew he couldn't explain any of it over an open channel, and he was bored of arguing. He knew now that even if he survived, he'd lose everything if the mission failed, but it was more important than any of it.

He reached the landing pad and found his comrades exactly where he had left them, except for Hughes. He looked to Waters for an answer.

"Gone to medical," he quickly answered before Taylor could open his mouth.

The rest of them were waiting for some explanation of what was going on, as only Jafar and Waters had any clue of the actions and revelations of the last few days.

"All right, listen up. Councillor Armand, you might have seen him on TV. He's a Krys agent, one of many, but the only one I know of for sure. We need him. He could well be the key to surviving whatever plan they have next to take this planet which we fought so hard for. He is the evidence of these enemy agents. Without him, they won't be able to operate among us without check."

"Let's nail the bastard then," replied Silva.

"We need him certainly, alive if at all possible, but here's the kicker, he's deep within UEN territory, exact location unknown at present. Despite what you did for me earlier today, we cannot fly military ships over the border and expect to be left alone to do what we need to do. I've got a bird coming, no idea what or how big, but it'll have to do. "

"You expect us to fly to war in some random piece of junk?" Rains asked.

"I expect you to improvise and overcome. This is what we have to do, so this is what we'll manage with."

"What sort of window do we have to find this guy?" asked Silva.

"Five hours."

"From when we get the ship?"

He shook his head.

"No such luck. I didn't say this would be an easy mission, but when do we ever get the easy ones? Our task is to find Armand, capture him, and bring him back to Meaux. That's it."

"Support?"

"Grey is being notified of our situation, Parker, but even if he does join our cause, he isn't gonna get here quickly. After we're over the border, we are on our own. No reinforcements, no support, and if we get trapped or captured out there, we're on our own."

"What do you mean trapped, Sir? It's only over the border."

He took a deep breath before the revelation that he was still trying to take in.

"We have five hours because that is the time frame before war is declared by the Alliance against UEN. Either way, we'll be foreign soldiers on sovereign soil. If we're assumed to be with the Alliance after that time, we'll be enemy combatants."

"And getting this guy is really as important as you say?"

"Absolutely, Parker."

"And we're the only chance of getting him before all this kicks off?" asked Silva.

"Yes. Now I have to say, anyone who wants out, leave now because once this kicks off, I need to know who I can depend on."

None responded, but he looked to Waters. He was not one of them.

"You're not a rifleman. I don't expect you be a part of this."

"I'm a part of this now. I'm no marine, but I'm one more fighter than you've currently got."

"Well, all right then."

All in. It's a start.

"Okay, I'm off to chase a few contacts and get a line on where we can find this Armand bastard. For those of you who don't know, he killed Tsengal, or had him killed at least. There's nothing I'd rather do than to ring his neck, but that is not what we are going to do. Alive at any cost! He'll suffer plenty worse in the long run, anyway. We leave as soon as our ride arrives. I suggest you use the time to gather any ammunition you can and get some chow!"

They split up to go about their business. Taylor wanted nothing more than to rest his aching body. He walked over to the shade by a small storage building, slumping there on the hard ground. He took off his helmet and put it down as he stretched out his legs. Parker was approaching. She kicked his feet until he looked up at her.

"Days ago you were bitching about having to fight a few Mechs. Now you're leading troops in to fight in combat, and against humans no less. What changed?"

"We have a reason to fight. Not for entertainment or recruitment, or any of that shit. But a reason like we had back in the wars."

"But it's not, is it? You can dress it up all you like, but then we had ironclad aliens coming at us. It was kill or be killed. But now the enemy is human."

"Or it looks human."

"When this starts, we're gonna be fighting humans, and you know it. Both these Krys agents and others who are little more than misguided."

"What do you want from me?

"To know what you want out of all this? Where are you going with it?"

He had to think about it for a moment.

"Wherever I have to for the survival of our people."

"But what does that mean for you? As soon as we won peace, you looked for another war. What are you fighting to achieve?"

"To fight for everyone else, I guess."

"And what about us?"

"We'll just have to wait. Let's not forget we signed up for this, both of us."

She couldn't argue with that, but she wanted to. She sat down beside him, and it was at least a relief for both of them to enjoy a peaceful moment together. A few minutes later that peace was broken. Silva threw down a box of ammunition before them.

"Load up," he ordered.

From any other NCO, Taylor would have taken it as an insult, but he nodded in gratitude. As he loaded his magazines, Rains strolled over, still looking uncomfortable and unimpressed.

"See that bird?" he asked. "One of the finest flying machines the World has ever known, and you want me to leave her on the ground and take God knows what to war?"

"That about covers it, yeah," replied Taylor.

As he said it, dust kicked up around them, and an aircraft descended. Rains looked around, and his shoulders slumped.

"You've got to be fucking kidding me."

The craft was at least forty years old and had clearly been used for tourism, as the signs of the tour operator were still partially in tact along the fuselage.

"Come on, Colonel," pleaded Eddie. "I've flown you to hell and back, but all I ask is you don't make me fly a coffin."

The craft came to a rough landing, but the undercarriage held firm. The pilot stepped out and strutted up to the Colonel to address him. Taylor was speechless as the man opened his mouth.

"She doesn't look like much, Colonel, but she'll get you across the border and won't attract any attention. She's called Adrienne, and she's been travelling northern Europe for decades."

"No shit," Eddie added.

"I know the owner, Sir. He says you can depend on her."

"To do what, give us a quick death?"

"All right, Rains," said Taylor, leaping up to the delivery pilot. "Thank you, we'll take her."

The man left as quickly on foot as he had arrived by air, but it wasn't the last he had heard of Rains.

"Come on, Mitch, I'm all up for this, but in that heap of junk? It's suicide!"

"Yeah, well, we've been through worse and made it out."

"But…"

"But nothing!" he yelled.

Rains was silenced and surprised at his sharp response.

"I know this sucks, but we're on the clock here, and this is our only chance. I asked you twice if you wanted to leave, and I'll only ask once more. We're gonna have to go through a whole load of crazy before this is over, so this is the last time, are you with me?"

He looked to Rains who turned and gave the ship another once over. He paced up to it. They were all silent, watching him run his hand down the bow of the ship. It was twice the size of one of their copters and obviously a clumsy beast.

"It has a little charm, at least," he replied.

Taylor smiled. He knew the hard sell had been made.

"Right then, load up. We're moving out!"

CHAPTER ELEVEN

Taylor stood over Rains as he powered up Adrienne, and they began to lift off the ground. The ship shook a little, and her engine exhaust ports crackled in a way that made Eddie grit his teeth and wince.

"Never thought I'd see the day where you wanted me to fly a coffin to war," he said.

"She ain't so bad. She's got character, you have to admit."

"Oh, yeah, character certainly, just no positive qualities. This is one old girl falling apart at the seams. She should be laid to rest at a junk yard, or maybe donated to a trailer park."

Taylor smiled. Rains' whining always entertained him. He turned and looked to the other copter crews that had come to his aid, now sitting as passengers the same as the rest of them. They carried carbines from their craft but had no armour to speak of.

"Your job is to guard this bird wherever you go, got it?"

They looked as suspicious of the ship as of Taylor, but nodded in acceptance.

"Yes, Sir."

Silva and Parker stepped up beside him. They were now clearly looking to him for answers.

"We'll split what we have into three squads. I'll take first, Silva, second, Parker you get third. I'll leave it to you to organise."

"Yes, Sir, but what about the mission?"

"What about it, Silva?"

"You got any idea how we're gonna find this Armand?" asked Parker.

"I know someone who can help. Just waiting to hear back."

"Bit of a long shot, don't you think?" asked Silva.

"You should be used to it by now. We lived on long shots during the war."

He shrugged. It was hard to disagree.

"Sir, we're coming up on the border. What do you want me to do?" asked Rains.

"Stay well away from the north and Belgium, cross near Saarbrucken, and remember, this is a civilian transport. Follow no military protocols, and give no implication of them either. That shouldn't be too hard for you."

"No, Siree."

"You think they'll just let us cross over?"

"There have been open borders here for a few hundred years, Parker. Until war is declared, I see no reason for that to change."

"Apart from France departing the UEN?" asked Silva.

Taylor shrugged. He could only hope they'd make it through.

Rains looked back at them.

"What's our story for being here?"

"University sightseeing."

"War's breaking out, and you think that story will hold?"

"That war hasn't broken out yet. As far as most people are concerned, this is just the usual strife in the World. Until it hits their doorsteps, they won't pay it much heed. If they do thermal identity checks as we pass by, I want it to look right we having this many aboard and little cargo."

"Sir, we got a call coming in," replied Rains, "It's anonymous and secure."

"Put it through to my pad."

Taylor lifted up the device and accepted the call. A projection appeared before them of a UEN officer they all recognised, Lukas Becker. But gone were his Captain's pips, replaced with a single one wrapped with a laurel.

"Major?" asked Taylor, "Congratulations on the promotion."

"And yours, Colonel, but shall we get down to business?"

"Certainly."

"You are the last person I expected to hear from at this time, and your recent stints in the World news have not endeared you to many hearts. And yet, out of the blue, I get a request from you that is most bizarre, and to fulfil would be a complete breach of my duty. Would you like to expand any further?

"I wish I could explain it all in a way which would make some sense and you could believe, but honestly I can't. You know me Becker, and you know where my loyalties lie. What I am telling you, is the information I need from you is vital in maintaining the defence of Earth from future conflict."

"And what of this conflict growing now?"

"It's all linked. I know it's crazy, all of it, but you'll just have to trust me."

Becker shook his head. They both knew it was asking a lot.

"You want the location of a high ranking government official of my country, and I can only imagine that means you want to either kill or kidnap him, because it surely is not for a conversation."

Taylor nodded in agreement. "It's not about loyalty to one's country any more, Becker, but loyalty to Earth and the human race."

"And if I do this for you, and my involvement is ever known, it will be the end of my career; the end of my life. I'll be behind bars till the day I die."

"I promise you that if we do not succeed in getting hold of Armand, your life will be over soon enough, anyway."

"You're expecting a lot of faith, based on little information or fact."

"Yes, and that's all I can tell you at this point. You know I'd do anything to protect this world. You know me. I'd only come to you with such a big ask if there was no other way."

"And if I say no?"

"I can't force you to help, but if you don't, well... I guess we're fucked."

Becker looked away as he thought about it. Taylor could see Parker watching anxiously to his side.

"Come on, Major, you're our only hope," Silva pleaded.

He finally looked up to address Taylor.

"Colonel, a lot has been asked of me, by you and many countless others over the last few years, but nobody has ever asked me to betray my country. I'll give you the information you ask for because I trust you, but do not let me regret it, or God help me, I will claw my way out of whatever hell I am imprisoned and chase you to the end of the galaxy."

Taylor smiled back. "Glad to see we understand one another. There'll come a time where we stand beside one another in combat again, Major. Sooner than you think, I suspect."

"All right. Councillor Armand is currently at an isolated

schloss in the mountains near Mittenwald."

"Schloss?" asked Parker.

"Like a castle or something?" Silva joined in.

"Yes, that kind of thing," replied Becker, "I have heard of this facility in the past year. Nobody I ask about it seems to know exactly what goes on there. Clearance is required to go there. Clearance from above my grade."

"What are you saying this place is?"

"Honestly, Colonel, I do not know. It is simply called Schloss Mittenwald, despite being a number of kilometres from the town. I am not entirely sure what it used to be before this title. Little attempt has been made to hide its location, only what goes on inside."

"Do you know anything about it at all?"

"Sorry. Any contacts I ask about it have nothing more to add, but many are suspicious about what goes on there."

"Why?"

"Ships regularly visit the Mittenwald, but nobody has any idea why, but…"

"But what, Major?"

"…I don't know. I hear strange things about the place, rumours, and each time different. Nobody seems to know for certain, but I don't like the sound of the place. I'd avoid it at all costs."

"Negative. If Armand is there, that's where we're heading. Thank you for this, Major. But I must now ask you forget it all. At some distant day in the future we may we meet and answer all of each other's questions, but until that day, protect yourself. We never had this conversation. You do not support the ideals of Mitch Taylor, and you don't go looking into this Mittenwald place, you hear me? I've lost enough friends over the years. You stay safe."

"I hope you are wrong about the Councillor. I pray that you are wrong, Colonel. But if you are correct, then good luck, and may we meet again in happier times."

The transmission ended, and Taylor dipped his head, feeling the heavy burden placed upon them all. He turned and looked to see that most of the marines had heard the conversation and were looking to him for answers.

"So here we are, at the point of no return. We cross that border and we're enemy combatants. It's gonna be dangerous, no doubt. You know what we're after, and you have some idea of how vital it is. Are you still with me?"

"Sir, yes, Sir!" they screamed.

It was all he needed to hear. He turned back to Rains who already knew what he was about to ask.

"We're passing over the border now. I have submitted our flight logs and declared our intentions."

"Think they'll buy it?"

"A few weeks ago, sure. Now, we can only hope."

Taylor looked out of the cockpit at the border, but there were no unique characteristics dividing the countries, much like crossing a state border back home. They all waited silently. Taylor half expected to be shot down, but as he held his breath, they passed over without any drama.

"Welcome to Germany!" yelled Eddie.

It was a small relief.

"How close can you get us to this schloss?"

"Area is a popular tourist destination, so I reckon with the flight path we put in, we can get within a few clicks before they start asking questions."

"Good, then set a path for a location that does not draw attention. You can divert to the schloss at the last possible moment, and bring us in low."

"That's it? That's the great plan?"

"Can't say we had months to plan this one, Eddie. We're doing what we have to do to get the job done."

"Which means putting my ass in the firing line, as usual?"

"Damn right, but you only have to get us there. It's the rest of us who have to go down and get the job done."

"Hell, yeah, I just do the flying."

The rest of the journey seemed to take hours. They sweated it out, expecting to be shot out of the sky at any moment. In reality, it was a short journey, even in the old hulk barely managing to stay in the sky.

"You know if it was anyone else, we'd say you were crazy?"

"I wish I was, Eli," he replied dryly.

More than anything, he wished he had the support of the Inter-Allied troops that fought beside him during the war, but this day, he commanded just a single platoon.

"You'll be taking Corporal Riley with you as your second-in-command," said Parker.

Taylor looked over, and the Corporal nodded in acknowledgement. Taylor hadn't seen him since soon after Demiran's fall in North Africa. Riley's skin was as dark as a human could be, and he stood a good head height over the Colonel. Taylor had known him since he was a fresh recruit and had never paused to share a word with the man. He bore a scar along the line of his chin and reaching up to his mouth, with burn marks still healing on his cheek. Gone was the rookie Taylor had known, replaced by a hardened veteran the likes of which Inter-Allied had become famed for.

"We got much of a plan?" asked Silva.

Taylor rubbed his forehead as he thought it over, but he couldn't lie to them.

"We're going in with no intel, and no idea of what we face. I can't say there's much of a plan beyond get in there and seize Armand. Fire only if fired upon. I don't want to kill a single human, but I will if I must. As you all must. Powers operate on this World the likes of which none of us fully understand. All that matters here is we get Armand, you get me?"

They all nodded. The tone had changed now. They were bearing down on a kind of war none of them had ever wanted and had long forgotten they had ever trained for; war against humans.

"ETA two minutes, Colonel! You sure you want to do this, now? Once we start this, God knows what kind of hell we're gonna bring down on ourselves!"

"That's beyond our control now. I figure we got about thirty to forty minutes before any reinforcements come our way. It'll be the last thing they expect, so we can only hope they aren't prepared for it."

"And if they are ready and waiting?"

"Let's just hope they ain't."

The last few moments passed quickly as they banked hard and headed for the Mittenwald schloss. Twenty seconds later a transmission came in. It was in English but with a strong German accent.

"Unidentified transport, you are approaching controlled air space of the UEN armed forces. Please alter course immediately."

Rains turned, looking to Taylor for answers.

"Tell him anything to buy time."

"This is the Adrienne. We're experiencing some problems with flight controls and cannot alter course. We've got nothing but students on board and are looking for a safe place to out down if we can."

The line went quiet for a moment. They all waited for the response, which finally came.

Adrienne, you are cleared to pass over Schloss Mittenwald at your current course and put down two clicks east of our position. Local emergency services will aid you on arrival."

"Uhhh, thanks Mittenwald, appreciate it."

Taylor smiled. He knew no other pilot could have sounded as confused and convincing as a civilian in distress, but Rains' acting himself pulled it off perfectly.

"Thirty seconds!"

"On your feet!" cried Taylor.

The marines jumped at his order, but they looked no less keen to do what needed to be done.

"Remember this is like every other mission we ever did. We'll get it done, and we'll get out alive!"

They felt the reverse thrusters kick in and splutter as they began to slow. A voice came over the comms again.

"Adrienne, continue on your current course, or you will be fired upon."

They came to a hover, and Taylor pulled open the door.

"Another day in the Corps!"

Without another word, he leapt from the door into the open air. As he began to free-fall, the first thing that struck him was the beautiful scenery, vast cavernous valleys along the southern border of Germany and over into Austria. They were jumping into combat, and yet all around them seemed at peace. He looked up to see the others were close behind him, but as the last marine was at the door, a missile soared up from a hidden location below.

The Adrienne took evasive action, but the missile

clipped the side of the hull and exploded. Taylor watched in horror as the ship soared off into the distance with smoke pouring from her.

"Rains get out of there!" he screamed down the comms.

There was no response. He saw the ship vanish between two peaks in the distance and could only hope for the best.

"Good luck, Eddie," he whispered.

His boosters kicked in, and he looked down. He was descending gently to the top of a rocky outcrop beside a vast structure. Dust bellowed out around his feet, and he could see the building before them was far from what he had expected.

From a distance it appeared to be hundreds of years old. Up close, it was of modern materials and only designed to appear the way it did to fool those from afar.

"Well, I'll be damned," said Silva, "Hell of a place to live."

They looked up. The wall was almost twenty metres high. Only half of the marines had hit the ground, but Taylor was already leaping back into the air with his boosters. He landed down on the edge of the roof, and an automated gun rotated to take aim at him. He turned quickly and fired. The domed mount jammed, and he put a few more rounds through it to be certain.

"Charges!"

"Two of his squad slapped magnetic charges down onto the steel roof and took cover. The explosion rocked the rooftop below their feet. Taylor jumped to his feet to see a metre-wide hole burrowed in the roof.

"Damn, that's serious armour!" Riley called out. Two more explosions ripped through the rooftop further along, and Mitch looked up just in time to see Parker jump in through the breach without any fear or hesitation. He wanted to be with her, but he knew the mission must come first before all else. He leapt forward and into the hole. As he hit the floor, a pulse struck his chest armour, and another zipped past his shoulder. He responded quickly by lifting his rifle and firing two shots at his attacker.

The dust was settling. They had jumped right into a guard station where an operator manned security feeds throughout the building. He looked down at the lifeless body of the man. It was the first human life he had ever taken. Taylor had never thought for a moment about striking a man, or even shooting those who deserved it, but shooting to kill one left him cold and feeling a little sick.

It was in this moment, he truly realised this was the sort of war he'd read so much about; the wars that had turned men crazy, and yet he'd always wished for. Riley landed beside him and was as fixated on the body as he was.

"Is this is what it's come to?"

"I wish I could say otherwise, but we must do what we have to do."

He stepped up to the console and looked at the screens

that displayed cameras all around the facility.

"Goddamn place is huge," said Riley.

"Yep."

"Shit."

Taylor looked at where Riley was pointing and spotted the unmistakeable outline of a Mech standing guard in one of the corridors. It was fully kitted in the armour they had seen during the war but carried a weapon resembling the Reitech equipment they used.

"They really are using Mechs?"

"Yeah, and that's just the start of it. Come on, Riley."

He rushed out the corridor, half expecting to find a line of Mechs, but it was quiet.

"Where are the guards?"

"We're not at war, remember. I bet they only got a skeleton crew guarding this place. Let's seize the opportunity while we still can."

He started a countdown on his watch of thirty minutes. Thirty minutes to find a single man within a complex they had no plans for or idea of his location. He heard an explosion in the distance and knew it would be Silva breaching on his right flank. He carried on forwards as an alarm sounded. It rang out through the entire complex.

As they reached the end of the corridor, it opened out into a hangar bay with a number of small aircraft laid up within a fully enclosed and sealed space. It was hidden from the air.

"That's the Councillor's ship."

He instantly recognised the lavish vessel he had recently travelled aboard. It was a relief to see some evidence of Armand's presence. It wasn't that he didn't trust Becker, but the information he had to offer seemed vague and bizarre.

A few mechanics were working on a ship nearby and turned to look at him and the others. But it wasn't Jafar they stared at, obviously used to Mechs, but him. They made no attempt to draw weapons. They simply ran.

"Nice to see it's not just me they fear now," stated Jafar.

Taylor rushed to Armand's ship and up the ramp to get on board. There was not a soul in sight. Reaching the cockpit, he knew it was an opportunity to ensure it stayed grounded. He targeting the cockpit console and fired a half dozen shots through the controls until they were completely fried. He left the ship as quickly as he had entered it and was surprised to see all was still quiet.

"I don't like this. Where are the guards?"

As he said it, a shot flew past his head and ricocheted off the hull of the ship.

"Careful what you wish for, Sir!" Riley yelled, as they leapt for cover.

Taylor advanced across under the cover of the ships and other equipment until he reached the doorway where the shots were coming from. Without sticking his head out, he armed a grenade and tossed it around the corner. He heard screams of panic, human screams, as the explosion rang out. He lifted his rifle to take the bend.

One soldier lay dead and another incapacitated beside him. Riley reached Taylor's side and was as shocked as the first casualty they had inflicted.

"How do we know these are the bad guys?"

"We don't, but they're fighting for them. Right now, it's collateral damage that we'll just have to live with."

The wounded soldier tried to reach for a pistol, and Taylor quickly responded with a shot to his head just beneath the helmet rim, killing him instantly.

"I didn't sign up for this."

"It's precisely what you signed up for and what we trained for. When in the Corps, did we ever train for alien invasion? No, we trained to fight our own kind. It ain't pretty, but it's what it is."

"What was the point of fighting if we were just gonna go back to fighting each other? We could have a world war on our hands if this continues."

"That's out of our hands now. We may be fighting humans, but this is as much a war started by the Krys as the last two. You don't have to like it. You just have to win."

"At what cost?"

"Enough questions. We get through this, and we might actually have a hand in what's going on and how to stop it."

He looked up and could see a junction up ahead.

"What I wouldn't give for a map of this place," he muttered.

They had no choice but to continue on, as he knew the other two squads would be doing. Gunfire echoed down through the junction they were approaching. Parker had found trouble, but there was no time to turn and help. He carried on at a steady pace with his rifle held at the ready.

The floor began to slope down and then turn as the gradient increased. They were going deeper now into the complex that must have been built into the rock of the mountain.

No way out now, you bastard, Armand.

They seemed to go about ten metres down until it levelled out. Taylor froze when a wall of Mechs met them. As they lifted their weapons to fire, he found an open doorway beside them and leapt in. The others were quick to follow, but the last was hit hard by two shots and stumbled as he came through. Jafar got a hold of him and hauled him inside. Taylor had only a brief second to look back and see the shots had hit his armour and the side of his leg.

"You have to stay on your feet!" he ordered the wounded marine.

Riley took a quick look at the wound. "It's gone right through. You'll be fine."

They were in some kind of scientific workshop or

laboratory.

"Take cover!"

Even over the sound of the alarm, they could hear the lumbering steps of the heavily armoured Mechs. It was a moment of nostalgia Taylor could have done without. He turned to see they were boxed into the room and could only hope there weren't too many coming for them. He jumped behind a metre-high metal workbench and lifted his rifle to the ready. He expected the Mechs to enter at any moment, mercilessly and without fear as they always had done, but what happened next was not what he was expecting at all. A flash grenade was launched through the entrance, and he had just enough time to yell, "Grenade!"

He ducked down for cover. The room was filled with light, and despite his best efforts, he was still hit by the shock of it. His ears were ringing, as he brought his rifle to bear but wasn't quite recovered. He fired two shots at the first Mech coming through the door, but they didn't come close to their target. Shots hit the top above him, and he was forced to duck back down.

His eyes were stinging and his vision blurred. His hearing was equally impaired, and he could taste the coarse chemicals that made up the grenades they had so often practiced with in training exercises before the war. He coughed and tried to get some air back in his lungs, but his mouth was dry. He looked up just in time to see a rifle barrel.

A burst of gunfire rushed over his head, and the rifle was dropped and fell over onto him. He could then see Jafar firing repeatedly. Mitch put his elbow up onto the worktop and hauled himself up with everything he had and brought his weapon to bare.

Erratic gunfire was smashing the doorway where the Mechs were trying to get through, and as many rounds were hitting them as were striking the wall. He got the last remaining enemy soldier in his sights and let rip with a burst of shots that riddled its body armour and all finally went still. His hearing was starting to come back, but it was met with the rather unnerving alarm buzzer going repeatedly. He tried to shake off the drowsiness, but it wouldn't budge. He got to his feet and almost stumbled over again. Jafar grabbed a hold of him and held him upright. He looked around and could see he'd been closest to the blast and was glad to the others were in far better shape than him. He gratefully took Jafar's arm to support him.

"Riley, lead on," he muttered.

Jafar hauled him over the bodies of the dead Mechs. When he got into the corridor, he started to get his balance back.

"Whose clever bloody idea was this?"

"That'd be yours, Sir," replied Riley.

The Corporal took the lead and was quickly engaged in gunfire at the next turn that Taylor was glad to sit out from. He looked at his watch. Five minutes had passed, and they were making slow progress.

"We have to keep moving forward!"

He looked in through a doorway to another room and could see exactly what they needed, a few Reitech shields. They seemed to be experimental models, but they'd have to do.

"Get those damn shields in there and drive forwards!"

Three marines each grabbed one of the devices and rushed to Riley's aid. They passed him, advancing as a steel wall down the corridor. Shots bounced off the thick armour. Mitch was finally getting back to normal, slammed a new magazine into his rifle, and rushed out to join the rest of them. They passed three Mechs who were smoking on the floor but more were still firing up ahead. They reached a bend and could hear someone shouting.

"Human, good, I want one alive."

"Why?" Jafar asked.

"Because it's about time we got some information on Armand's whereabouts."

"And they would give it to you?"

"I intend to be persuasive."

He looked out and saw the human was an officer working with two Mechs.

"Advance, but keep him alive!"

The shield bearers rushed out and stormed down the corridor. One struck a Mech with a barge; another used his shield to drive the Mech's weapon up and out the way, firing several shots into its legs. It collapsed, and he put one through the faceplate.

Taylor was in quickly, but the officer had already thrown down his rifle to surrender.

"Armand, where is he?"

The man shook his head. Taylor drew out his pistol and fired a shot through the officer's foot. He screamed and collapsed in agony, but Taylor wasn't done with him. He grabbed him by his helmet, unclipped the straps, and ripped it from his head.

"Armand, where is he?"

"I don't know!"

Taylor spun his pistol around and clubbed the man's jaw with the grip, causing blood to spew out across the wall he was lying against. Riley was shocked, but he did nothing to stop the Colonel.

"I'm running out of time, and I'm willing to do whatever I have to here. I don't want to kill you, but your life is not more valuable than our task here. Tell me where we will find Armand, and I promise you no more harm will come to you."

The man coughed out blood and turned to look at the crazy expression in Taylor's eyes, realising he wasn't kidding around.

"Live or die, your choice."

"Conference room at the lowest level."

"What's he doing there?"

"I don't know!"

"There must be another way out from this place!"

When he didn't get a response, Taylor lifted the pistol, once again threatening a strike.

"There is, there is!" he cried, "There's an access corridor from beneath the compound. It leads to emergency escape shuttles in a hidden area of the mountain to the east."

"How long does it take to get there?"

"From here, five minutes, maybe. Please, I don't want to die."

"And I don't want to kill you. Do not make any more attempts to harm me and mine, and you'll make it out of here alive."

The man seemed surprised.

"But you're Taylor, the Butcher. You don't leave your enemies alive!"

"Then don't be my enemy."

It was yet more evidence of the distain and resentment that was being felt towards him. He could only think it was as a result of carefully targeting campaigns against him, as well as Weaver's idiotic schemes. He was now starting to wonder if Weaver had been one of the enemy agents like Armand, but it didn't bear thinking about.

"How do we get to the conference room?"

"Just carry on the way you were going. It'll take you there."

"And this secret landing pad?"

"Only accessible from a room marked as Storage 24B, or through the outside landing doors which are completely hidden until open."

"Then we'd better move. I won't kill you, but neither can I let you spill the beans."

Taylor smacked the man across the head with his pistol, knocking him unconscious.

"How can we make it before Armand flies outta here?"

"We run, Riley, and we hope," replied Taylor. He jumped forward and carried on at a pace far beyond safe when they were in such proximity to the enemy.

He lifted up his comms unit. "Eddie, are you okay?"

"Yep, just about!"

"Bring Adrienne around to the east side of the mountain, ASAP!"

"Got any co-ordinates on that?"

"No, I don't. Just do it, and be ready to give pursuit!"

"In this piece of junk?"

"We're running out of options. Armand might be leaving shortly from a hidden landing area on the east side. You must not let him leave. Just make it work!"

"You got it," he responded wearily.

"Any craft they have will outpace the Adrienne, surely?"

"Sure will, Riley."

They carried on deeper into the facility, finding no resistance for several minutes. They finally arrived at a broad atrium that was clearly the entrance to something important; the conference hall they had been looking for. He could see two Mechs guarding the door, but they did not have time to take cover. Taylor's rifle opened up, as did several others beside him. The two Mechs frantically tried to return fire and got off a few wild shots as they were bombarded by a salvo from the marines. There was a keypad security system to get in, but the doors didn't look all that strong. Mitch fired a few shots into the pad and then the centre locking mechanism before getting his fingers through a small hole he'd blasted.

The door began to open ever so slowly when out of nowhere Jafar came thundering in against the other door, bursting through with little resistance at all. The steel door was launched into the room. The rest of them were left speechless.

"Come in!" he called.

They rushed through the breach and could immediately see a doorway at the far side of the room. It had been left open in haste.

"We can't be far behind, go!" Taylor ordered.

As he passed along the length of the table, he noticed a number of documents scattered across it, the kind only kept in hard copy for security reasons. He wanted to stop and take what he could but knew they did not have a moment to spare.

The door ahead led to a square corridor of three metres

wide. It ascended relatively gently in an almost straight line.

"Faster!" He got to a sprinting pace, knowing Armand wouldn't have a suit on that would allow the kind of pace they could manage. He hoped it would be enough. As they were reaching the top, they could see evidence of daylight and could hear an engine power up.

"Shit," Taylor muttered.

They reached the very top and broke out into the landing zone. It stored just three small high-speed shuttles. One of them had got a metre of the ground. Mitch looked to the two spare craft in the hope of taking one, but could already see bullet holes through the turbine housings.

"Rains! Stop that ship!"

"With what, Colonel?"

He lifted his rifle and took careful aim at Armand's ship. It was beginning to gain forward momentum. He squeezed the trigger and fired off three well-aimed shots at one of the two engines. He lowered his rifle and watched in hope. The pulsing engine spluttered and began to die. He knew he had done it.

"Nice shooting!" Riley said as he reached the landing pad beside Taylor.

"It's not enough. He's still getting away."

Engines roared above them, and the Adrienne lowered down twenty metres from the rock edge. The side door was open and one of Eddie's fellow pilots at the door.

"Come on, jump!"

Riley looked over the edge. It was a several thousand-metre drop. He knew the boosters on his suit should keep him safe, but that wasn't enough to make him feel sick to the stomach.

"Uhhh… Colonel," he began to hesitate.

He turned around. Taylor had gone back a way to get a run up.

"What? D'you wanna live forever?"

He ran, using the power of his suit go forwards into the wide doorway of the ship and landed rather ungraciously. He tumbled over into a roll, coming to a rest on one knee.

"Come on!"

"Oh, what the hell," muttered Riley. He took a running jump and launched out into the sky. He had underestimated the distance slightly and struck the lower edge of the entrance to the hatch. Taylor jumped forward, sliding across the deck on his front. He came out slightly over the edge and took a firm hold of one of Riley's arms. He looked down just for a moment at the rocky crag below and realised how close they had come to death, but it was too late to go back now.

Taylor hauled Riley on board. The others were already leaping in, having learnt from his experience. Taylor yelled into his comms.

"All aboard, after that bastard!"

CHAPTER TWELVE

"Chase him down!"

"I'm trying!" Rains shouted.

Taylor could just about see Armand's ship in the distance. They weren't losing them, but neither did they appear to be making any progress.

"Eddie, we don't get him, and this was all for nothing."

"I don't know what to tell you, Colonel, not like we have any weapon systems to slow them down any further."

"This thing going all out?"

"Bet your ass. It's a goddamn miracle she keeps going."

"My shot did some damage to one of their engines. How come we aren't gaining on them?"

"Well you did some damage sure, but she's a high speed transport, and we're in the equivalent of the old school bus."

Taylor sighed and drooped his head. It felt like it was

all over.

"Wait, that turbine you hit, it's just lost all power. We're gaining on them!"

Cheers rang out from the marines behind.

"Wait, they're banking. Where the hell are they going?"

"They know they can't outrun us, so they're going for a place of safety. Local forces will already be scrambling. I'd say we got about fifteen minutes max until we're swamped."

"All right, so where are they heading?" asked Rains.

"Somewhere as secret as Mittenwald, somewhere with allied Mechs, somewhere with troops who would have no trouble gunning us down, not even if they knew who I was."

"Great, where is that?"

"We'll have to wait and see."

"In fifteen minutes? Cutting it a little fine, aren't we?"

"Love to say I had a better option."

"They're levelling off...and starting a descent."

"Stay with them. Follow them down and get on the ground ASAP."

Rains nodded in agreement.

"What is that place, Eddie?"

No idea, Colonel, just looks like another mountain to me."

"That ain't no mountain!" Riley screamed.

Lights pulsed below and anti aircraft flak burst around

them.

"No missiles?" asked Taylor.

"This ain't enough for you?" asked Eddie, as the craft shook from the impacts.

"Just makes me suspicious, is all."

"They aren't trying to shoot us down. They're trying to force us to turn back."

"Why?" he asked, but he already knew the answer.

"So they really don't want to kill us."

"Not that I don't want to believe that, but why?"

"A platoon of US Marines going down on UEN soil when war is about to break out. Armand will do anything to avoid bringing the US into this war."

"Yeah, well good luck with that."

"Don't knock it. That fact might just keep us alive to get this job done."

Taylor watched intently on the view screen as the shuttle landed roughly on a ledge of the mountain. As they ground to a halt, a number of figures rushed to their aid.

"Guess that's our target?" asked Eddie.

Taylor grunted in approval.

"They may not want to shoot us down now, but you know once we have the Councillor all bets are off, you know that right?"

"You just worry about flying this hulk, Eddie, and leave the fighting to us."

"Not much of a relief after there's another missile coming for my ass."

Taylor didn't know how to answer that as he knew it was an almost certainty. He turned to the others.

"They may not want to shoot us out of the sky, but once we're on the ground, armed foreign operatives, they will not hesitate to start shooting again!"

"Making a lot of assumptions aren't you?" whispered Parker.

"Only going on what we have seen so far. All I do know is we have to be fast about this."

"No shit."

Eddie brought them in as fast as he could and came close to overdoing it. The landing gear hit the ground hard, and they could feel it buckle a little as they slid a few metres to a halt.

"Goddamn miracle we weren't shot out the air."

"We're made of miracles, Eddie. We're the Immortals!"

He leapt out the side door of the ship without a word to the others. He knew they'd be close behind him. He wished he had a plan beyond jumping into the unknown, but there was no time. He hit the ground running despite the imminent danger, but was surprised to see not a single enemy in sight.

Taylor rushed first to the shuttle that had come to an even rougher landing than they had. He looked through the door that had been left open and found nothing. He looked out and around the site. They were on a small hidden landing zone on the side of a mountain in a seemingly tranquil hiking spot.

"Where the hell are they?" asked Riley.

"Must be somewhere more important than the Mittenwald. Armand would never risk revealing this place unless he had absolutely no choice."

"All right, but where?" asked Silva, "Nothing here but nature and us."

He looked down to the footsteps coming from the shuttle.

"Sergeant, time to go back to basics."

Silva looked down at the tracks and looked sheepish for not having gone to them sooner.

"Tracking not something we've had to do in years, not like finding the enemy was ever much of a difficulty."

"Say that again."

They followed four sets of tracks between some rocks until they finally found something else manmade, a thick steel double doorway, hidden by nature of its remote location and inability to see from the air.

"Explosives now, everything we have!" Taylor hollered.

A few of the marines passed magnetic charges forward, but it was all they had.

Five? That's it? Taylor thought.

He didn't let his doubt spread by voicing his mind and placed the charges quickly, with just a ten second delay to start simultaneously.

"Cover!"

He ducked behind a nearby boulder and prayed. The explosion erupted and rocked the ground beneath them. Taylor had become accustomed to constant ear splitting noise during the war, but he had always hoped in those moments for the survival of him and his comrades. But now all that was gone. Their lives were of no concern to him in that moment. He knew all that mattered was getting Armand.

He got up. The doors had completely vanished from sight. It was a welcome surprise to them all.

"Guess they weren't ever expecting the kind of guests who don't knock," Riley grinned.

Taylor went in first. It was a narrow corridor, the width of two humans. It looked like an emergency escape or access tunnel to a much larger facility. A red emergency light was pulsating along its length, and they knew it was in response to their arrival.

"I don't like this, Mitch."

"You and me both, Eli, so let's get it done quick."

He rushed into the breach, knowing the others would soon follow. The corridor soon split into a wide fork.

"Which way?" she asked.

Before any of them could answer, they were welcomed by gunfire from the right fork. Taylor raised his rifle, quickly fired two shots in return. And shouted.

"Left!"

He rushed on. The rest fired and did the same.

"Silva, you stay put and hold this position."

"You think we're gonna get back out of here?"

"Didn't come here to fail, Riley."

Taylor carried on through a doorway. It was pitch black for a moment as they all came to a halt. The red pulsing lights from the corridor provided a small insight as to what was before them. They saw silhouettes that were too large to be human. A moment later the lights were turned on, and several of the marines gasped at the sight in front of them. They were in some kind of training hall, and twelve full armoured Mechs stood there. They were holding shields like the Reitech ones they were accustomed to, only larger.

It was a small relief to see they carried Assegai derived weapons and no firearms, but that relief soon wore off. The creatures leapt into action and rushed towards them like a herd of wild animals.

"Oh, shit," muttered Taylor.

He lifted his rifle and fired a few shots, but the shields absorbed them all. There seemed no way to slow the charge down.

"Jump!" he cried in a panic.

He launched several metres off the ground and came close to the rooftop with the use of his boosters. Most of the marines jumped with him, but he could see Riley and a handful of them had stood their ground and continued to fire. As Taylor reached the apex of his jump, he fired down beneath his feet. Three shots went right down into the faceplate of the Mech he had targeted, and it collapsed to the floor, sliding up to Riley's feet.

Several others followed suit, but it wasn't enough to stop the charge. Three marines were struck full force and launched off their feet. Jafar had stood his ground with them and tackled one of their attackers head on, driving an Assegai right through one to deal a killing blow.

Taylor was back on his feet and had the enemy in his sight once again, but friendlies were now mixed in with the Mechs. He drew out his Assegai and rushed at them. One of the nearest creatures turned and thrust its shield out to strike him. He could only jump into a roll and hope to make it under. His shoulder armour brushed the lower edge as he just made it under, and sparks followed from the contact. He was back up on one knee with lighting speed and fired several shots before driving his Assegai up into the belly of the creature's armour.

The warm blue blood he had come to know so well flowed out over his hand. Gone was the regret and doubt he had felt in the arena. He was no longer fighting for sport or entertainment. He was fighting for everything. He turned to take on the next creature, but Parker was already jumping into action at the nearest target. She drove her weapon into the exposed joint beneath one of the Mechs' arms and followed the creature to the floor. She had a smile on her face as she turned to look at him. She was in her element, and so was he.

Taylor looked up. Riley was sitting against the wall, clearly unable to get up. Another marine lay dead beside him.

"You still able to fire that weapon, Riley?"

"Yes, Sir."

"Then you nail anything that comes through here that ain't one of our own, you hear?"

"Aye, aye, Sir."

Taylor got back on his feet. The marines had made light work of the rest of the enemy.

"Enough fun and games. We have a job to do!"

He looked down at his watch, only six minutes left on the timer he had set.

Cutting it awfully close.

They continued on through the room. It was clear to all of them from the equipment around that the Mechs they had fought had been in training.

God help us when they are fully trained, thought Taylor.

"How many more obstacles are we gonna have to face to get this bastard?" asked Parker.

"He's running scared. This welcome party wasn't prepared for us. It was a last minute deal, so we must be getting close."

They passed through into the next room that appeared

to be empty, but a glimmer of movement in one corner caused Jafar to rush across to engage whatever danger was there. As he arrived ready to fire, a human leapt up with her hands in the air. It was a scientist in a lab coat. She was almost frozen in fear, and tears streamed from her eyes. She could not find the breath to speak.

"Jafar!" yelled Taylor.

The alien turned in surprise.

"She's unarmed, a non-combatant."

He looked back at her for a moment, finally accepting Taylor's orders. He returned to the Colonel and spoke in no uncertain terms at a volume all could hear.

"Everyone in this building is a combatant."

"Not for you to decide, buddy, nor me. While there are still human laws in the land, we'll abide by them."

"Like kidnapping a Councillor on his home soil?"

Taylor glared at Parker. He already realised he was being hypocritical, but he didn't have time to rephrase his comment.

"All right, enough bullshit. Let's get this son of a bitch before this little holiday is the end of us."

Taylor led the way through another two rooms that were full of experimental equipment they didn't have the time to investigate, finally reaching a control room. It was large and filled with screens monitoring the facility. At a distance, Taylor could still just about see a few of the screens and frantic movement on them, which he already suspected were other troops in the facility gearing up to fight them.

"It's over, Colonel!" Armand shouted.

Taylor laughed. He noted the Councillor was now wearing a Reitech suit he had clearly hastily pulled on since their arrival. His suit was crumpled up beneath it, and the helmet was ill fitting and almost dropping over his eyes.

"You're coming with us, Councillor. Alive is preferable, but we'll take what we can get."

There were only three guards standing beside him, and one of those was clearly the pilot who had flown them there. Taylor turned his focus to address them.

"You can walk away from this. No need to die."

"These are soldiers loyal to me, Colonel."

He knew that meant they were either Krys agents, or deeply loyal to those who were. It was all the evidence he needed to condemn them. He lifted his rifle and fired two shots at the first, and his comrades quickly did the same. They hadn't even got their muzzles up before they were hit and had certainly never expected such violence.

"You forget who you are dealing with, Councillor."

"Evidently. Then let's do this man-to-man, the honourable way."

Taylor smiled as Armand picked up a shield and Assegai.

"We don't have time for this," muttered Parker.

"We can give the man his chance. It won't take long."

Taylor drew out his Assegai and approached. Against

any one of his own marines, he would fear opposing them without a shield when they were equipped with one. But against Armand, he didn't give it a moment's consideration. At first, the Councillor stepped forward uneasily, as if he were the kind of rookie who had never used the equipment before. It amused Taylor and caused him to approach without caution, but as he did so, Armand leapt into action like a different man altogether, like a trained soldier.

Taylor managed to jump aside in time to avoid a thrust that was coming to his face, but he was off balance. As a result, Armand struck him with the shield, and he stumbled across the room.

"Mitch!" cried Eli.

He regained his balance, cursed himself for being so foolish. He'd seen enough surprises in his life now to never throw caution to the wind, and yet he still did.

"Right, let's do this."

He rushed forward as if in a wild charge, stopping abruptly as Armand held his shield out to stop him, spun off to the side and smashed the weapon down on the inside of the man's knee. It buckled. The Councillor dropped down onto one knee and let out a scream of pain. The strike had been like nothing more than that of a baton as Taylor knew the edge did no more, but it provided immense satisfaction to see the pain in Armand's face.

"You're a traitor to your people, Councillor."

"You think you're my people just because we look alike!" he yelled, as he got back up and raced forward once more. He attacked quickly with repeated short stabs that were difficult to counter. They forced Taylor to give ground across the room. He was backed against a worktop and had to spin out from the attack.

"Why do you fight? You know you cannot win."

"But you always did. You and your Immortals went into many a fight you should never have been able to win, and yet here you are today. Standing before me and ruining things once more."

"Your monologuing bores me," replied Taylor.

Armand jumped forward once more as if to continue with his quick thrusts but used it only as a feint and drove his shield forward as a barge once again, but Taylor would not be caught off guard a second time. He caught the rim of the shield with his offhand and forced it forward, pulling Armand off his feet and launching him across the room. Taylor held a firm grip on the shield, wrenching it from the Councillor's grasp.

"You're coming with us, whether you like it or not."

Armand let out a roar of a battle cry and rushed at Taylor, launching a clumsy long lunge. Taylor stepped aside and took a hold of his arm. He drove a knee below the torso armour into Armand's abdomen. He keeled over. The weapon dropped from his grasp, and he was done for. Taylor wanted to feel some respect for the man having tried, but then he remembered all that he had done against his own people, against his own race.

"Your ass is mine now, Councillor."

"Mitch, we got incoming!" Parker shouted.

He looked over to the screens. Mechs and human soldiers were flooding towards them from other parts of the facility. He looked down at his watch, three minutes.

"Let's go, go, go!"

He smacked Armand in the face, knocking him unconscious, threw him over his shoulder, and took off back the way they came. As they burst out into the room where they had fought the line of Mechs, they found Riley still firmly planted against the wall with his rifle held ready to fire. Taylor didn't have to say another word. Jafar grabbed him, and another took the body of the fallen marine.

As they rushed into the corridor, they could hear a tonne of gunfire where Silva was clearly meeting some resistance where he had taken up position. Taylor didn't slow one bit, nor have a weapon to hand. He held onto Armand firmly with both hands and darted for the exit.

"Where the hell have you been?" Silva shouted. He slammed in a new magazine, and the rest of his squad kept up the fire.

"Getting the job done! Lay down fire till the last have gone by, and then get your ass out of here!"

"Hell, yeah!"

He turned the corner and kept firing. Taylor continued on and broke out into the daylight. It was the best sight he had seen all day and gave him a real sense that they could succeed in their mission. He didn't have to tell Rains anything, for the engines of the Adrienne were already running.

"All squads back to the boat. We are leaving!" he called down the comms.

The scene on the mountainside was eerily quiet and peaceful like when they had arrived, but they all knew it wouldn't last. Taylor was the first to reach the ship and jumped aboard to be sure Armand was secure. He kept a hand firmly locked on him.

"We got incoming, fast!" said Rains.

"Just a few more seconds."

"A few more seconds, and we'll be dead before we get off the ground!"

Taylor didn't respond. He looked out the door. Silva was the last man out, and as he reached the craft, a bullet went through his leg, and he dropped to the floor.

"Hold him!" Mitch bellowed to Parker, throwing the Councillor at her. He jumped out, took a hold of the Sergeant, and threw him in through the door. As he did, a bullet clipped his cheek and burnt the flesh, but he barely noticed in the rush to get out alive.

"Get us in the air!" he shouted before his feet had even

got off the ground.

The Adrienne lifted off, and he had to use a little of the power of his suit to launch him up into the doorway. Jafar pulled him in safe. Silva nodded in appreciation as he winced in pain.

"Look after the Councillor," he said to Jafar, "Parker, with me!"

They rushed to the cockpit as they heard a few shots being fired from the doorway.

"Can't believe we made it," said Parker joyfully.

"We ain't home yet."

They reached Rains, who was hoping and praying, as the ship was giving all it had to give. Taylor looked down at his watch. The timer had ended. It had been a pretty good estimate, but now they were in the shit.

"We got fighters incoming, and no, we can't outrun them."

"What do you suggest?" asked Mitch.

"Suggest? We're in a flying coffin. I suggest you pray for a miracle."

He waited for a moment and came close to doing exactly that.

"They've got a lock on us."

"You must be able to do something?"

"We ain't got speed, handling, weapons, armour, nothing. What can I do? Hang on, we have an incoming transmission."

Taylor thought there was hope for a moment while Eddie accepted it, only to be met by the face of a German fighter pilot.

"Adrienne, you are in UEN airspace and are ordered to alter course to land in Munich immediately."

Eddie gave no response, looking to Taylor for answers.

"I repeat, Adrienne, you are in violation of UEN treaties and are illegally holding a UEN Council member. You will be escorted to Munich airport immediately, or you will be fired upon."

"They'd blow us out the sky and kill Armand in the process?" asked Eddie.

"Instead of letting us get our hands on a known Krys agent, damn right they will. Remember Ramstein? Whole base flattened to protect this secret."

"Then I don't know what to say to you, Colonel, other than open the doors and jump. Your suits will get you down safe, and you can try and make it out on foot."

Taylor shook his head.

"No way, you've been with us through the worst of it. We're getting out of this together."

"Your sentiment is appreciated, Colonel, but it won't save any of us."

The fighter pilot came onto the screen once again.

"Adrienne, you have thirty seconds to alter course, or you will be shot down. Don't make us do this. There is no reason for further bloodshed."

The line went quiet for precisely twenty seconds.

"You have ten seconds to comply, nine, eight, seven, six, five, four, three, two, one…"

Everything went silent for a moment until a red light began to flash on the console, and a recorded voice message sounded.

"Warning, object on collision course."

It was repeated over and over.

"Hold on!" Eddie shrieked.

He banked as hard as the ship could, but it was a mild manoeuvre at best. One missile rushed past the hull. The other impacted and rocked them in the sky. Warning lights came up all over the console.

"We've got a breach. We're losing power!"

"How many more of those can we take?"

"I'm amazed we lasted after that one, Mitch. This old girl is built strong, but she won't take another!"

"You're just full of good news, Eddie."

"I can't do the impossible."

"How far back are those fighters?"

"About half a click on our tail."

He shook his head. He was all out of ideas. He closed his eyes and hoped, for there seemed nothing else to do.

"We got another two missiles incoming!"

They knew now they were on borrowed time with just seconds to live. It wasn't the first time Taylor had been there, but he couldn't see a way out of this one. He turned and looked to Armand who had been hauled into the cockpit and stripped of his armour. Before he could speak, the Councillor uttered words through a sleazy smile.

"You can never win, Taylor. This is the end for you."

"But you're going down with us, you son of a bitch."

"My life to take out the great Colonel Taylor. It would be worth a thousand lives to kill you."

"Ten seconds to impact. Hang on, what the hell's that?"

Taylor turned around and saw several missiles roar towards them and past the cockpit. A few seconds later, and six fighters zoomed past at full tilt. Explosions rang out at their aft where the enemy missiles exploded.

"Who the hell's that?" Taylor asked.

Rains brought up rear monitoring screens and squinted to make them out.

"Well, I'll be damned. Those are French birds."

They watched as the fighters engaged those on their tail and quickly blew them out of the sky. Taylor looked down at the map screen. They were just twenty clicks from the border now. One of the French fighters came alongside them and gave a casual salute before putting through a call on the comms.

"Adrienne, this is Lieutenant Roux. We're here to escort you back home."

Cheers rang out amongst the marines. They'd all overheard, as Rains had transmitted the signal throughout the ship. Taylor looked down at his watch.

"War can't have been declared yet," he muttered to himself. He turned to Rains.

"Can the Lieutenant hear us?" he asked. Rains nodded in response.

"Lieutenant, you just entered UEN airspace in an act of war."

"I am well aware of that, Colonel, but I am told you were worth the risk."

"I'd say so," he replied with a laugh.

"Just one more thing, Colonel."

"Yeah, go ahead."

"A message from General Dupont. He says you better have the package with you, or he'll shoot you himself."

Taylor could only laugh louder at the message.

"Then I am glad to be able to disappoint the General once more."

The pilot didn't seem to understand the meaning or context and replied sternly. "Maintain speed and follow my course."

"Do what I can," replied Eddie, "but we ain't got a lot of power left."

There was no response. The pilot took up position in front, and Eddie looked down. The rest of his wing had formed up all around them. Taylor turned back to Armand with a broad cheesy grin on his face.

"Once more we live to fight another day."

Armand looked away as it was clear he was utterly

defeated. But then he looked back up defiantly with anger in his eyes.

"You'll never get away with this. I am an elected representative of the UEN. They'll come down on you like a tonne of bricks. You'll wish you never met me, Taylor. You'll wish you'd met the same fate as your friend Tsengal, and Chandra, and all the other pathetic friends you have lost throughout these wars. I hope you survive long enough to see everyone you care for enslaved or killed."

Taylor sighed, thinking about the element of truth he spoke, but then nodded to Parker who knew exactly what he meant. She swung a hard punch into his stomach. He reeled over in pain from the injury Taylor had recently inflicted. She pulled him upright again, punching him hard in the nose so that it almost flattened to his face. It clicked as it broke, and blood poured out down his face and his suit. He cried out in pain.

"We're at war now Armand, and you are not an enemy combatant, not a civilian representative, and not a prisoner of war. No, you are a spy, and in turn we owe you no pleasantries. You'll see no court room."

Parker went to strike him once again, but Armand skilfully avoided the strike and ducked under, grabbing Parker's pistol from its holster as he did. He lifted the pistol up to his jaw to blow his head off. Before he could do so, Taylor's rifle was up, and he fired a single shot. It struck Armand's wrist and blew his hand off. He cried out in pain, but he found little sympathy. Parker looked sheepish as she picked up her gun and prised Armand's severed hand from it.

"Get that patched up," Taylor said, "and be sure to detain him. I want this son of a bitch alive after all the work we put in to get him."

"We're over the border and on the home run!" Rains suddenly shouted.

Further cheers rang out. It seemed almost unreal that they had made it out alive.

"It's over," said Eddie relieved.

"No, it's only just begun. We've got a new war on our hands, and we're gonna be fighting human on human."

"Why? Can't people see how crazy that is now?"

"Hasn't stopped them in the past."

As they approached Meaux, they heard the Adrienne's engines finally cut out, and they all knew it would come down hard. Rains was doing everything he could to slow them down and keep the nose up, but as they came down on the landing pad, they hit so hard it felt like the ship would tear itself apart.

The Adrienne bounced and then came down hard once again, slipping across the ground with sparks flying up on either side. After thirty metres of grinding along the strip, they finally struck a truck. The nose of the Adrienne pierced right through the bodywork of the vehicle and wedged itself there, bringing them to a halt. Rains looked around in shock that they were still in one piece.

"I tell you what, she may be an old girl, but she's a good 'un."

"Not that she'll ever fly again."

"Oh, come on, Colonel, have some heart. She got us through it all. I'm not ready to give up on her yet."

"You're a sentimental bastard."

"And you're just a bastard," he smiled.

Taylor grabbed Armand who was still cowering in pain. Parker had bound up his wound but had refrained from giving him any painkillers. They led him between them to the door on the side of the ship. They found Silva still sitting where Taylor had thrown him aboard.

"You all right?"

"I'll live."

Taylor hit the door release button but nothing happened, so he pulled down the override, but that was jammed also. With little finesse, he lifted his foot and kicked the door full force. It fell from its broken mounts and dropped to the ground. Fire crews and medics were already arriving on the scene, and Taylor could see the General's vehicle approaching at speed. Dupont was on his feet before the medics had even reached them. He stopped for a moment to look at the wrecked state of Armand. Blood and dirt covered much of his suit.

"When I said dead or alive, I didn't expect you'd meet

me half way," he said to Taylor.

"Best of both worlds, I guess."

Dupont stretched out his hand to him. It was a moment he never thought to see. He had to think about it for a moment, as their history was turbulent at best, but he accepted the gesture.

"You saved our asses up there. I can't thank you enough."

"And if this man is who you say he is, it was well worth it. Welcome back, Colonel."

The medics took Armand off their hands with the MPs close in tow.

"War will be declared within the hour. The United States is still remaining neutral, and your government is chasing for your return, but I will not send you back. I would be a fool to give away one of the greatest assets we have. If you are willing to stay here and fight for the European Alliance, then I will be honoured to give you a commission as such at your present rank."

Taylor stopped and looked back at his marines for a moment who were battle weary and exhausted. He knew they would go to hell and back if he asked them, and he knew he must.

"You're on, General."

"Then welcome to the European Alliance."

"This war we are starting, it is just the beginning. It is the Krys' doing, and Armand is proof of that. Jafar tells me it is a prophecy of theirs. They believe Earth is the paradise they must find and make their home. They will never stop coming for it. They failed to defeat us as a united world, now they seek to divide and conquer. A plan that so far seems to be going in their favour."

"But we have little choice at present but to fight the clear and present danger."

Taylor knew it was the last day of peace the World would know for some time. He hated the enemy invaders. He hated what they stood for and everything they strove to achieve over the human race, but he was now in his element once more, as a new Battle for Earth was beginning.

Engines roared overhead, and six ships landed just off to their flank.

"Friends of yours, I believe," said Dupont.

"The ramps dropped, and a familiar face rushed out from the nearest ship, leading a group of British paratroopers he had come to know as his closest friends and allies.

"Captain Grey reporting for duty, Sir!"

Two hundred troops formed up before them, all equipped and under his command.

"Welcome to the European Alliance and the new Inter-Allied Regiment!" yelled Colonel Mitch Taylor.

THE END